Machi Goes Viral...

Choose Your Friends Wisely!

Shveta Iyer

INDIA • SINGAPORE • MALAYSIA

ISBN 979-8-89984-783-7

A CUTE LOVE STORY.

"Stranger-Bestfriend-Stranger"

Choose your friends wisely!

“The right one stays”
– Shveta Iyer

Contents

About the Author

Shveta Iyer is an accomplished author and artist with a Bachelor of Fine Arts (B.F.A.) degree from the prestigious Sir J.J. Institute of Applied Art, Mumbai. A true creative soul, Shveta wears many hats. She is a freelance interior designer, yogini, traveler, health enthusiast, actor, model, biker, and photographer. Her passion for writing shines through in her soulful reflections on love and uplifting quotes about life.

In **2022,** she debuted her **first solo art exhibition,** *Lockdown Stories*, featuring medium-line artworks at **Jehangir Art Gallery, Fort, Mumbai.** That same year, she showcased her **second solo exhibition** of black-and-white self-portrait photography at **NCPA, Nariman Point, Mumbai.**

In **2023,** Shveta's work reached an international audience through an art exhibition at **Cloudscape Art Gallery in Manila, Philippines.**

In **2024,** she authored her first book, ***"Hazaribagh: City of One Thousand Gardens",*** focused on women's empowerment. The book received widespread appreciation from renowned Political and Bollywood personalities for its powerful message and artistic expression.

Shveta has also appeared in national television commercials and is a proud Royal Enfield Bullet rider, making her a symbol of strength and freedom for many aspiring women riders. In her free time, she finds joy in teaching drawing to children, using creativity as a tool for connection and growth. She believes,

> *"Life is a beautiful gift, stay positive, spread love, encourage the next generation, and work hard until your dreams come true."*

Through her work, both visual and written, Shveta Iyer continues to inspire others with her passion, resilience, and unwavering optimism reminding everyone that the seeds of hope and effort we plant today will blossom into joy tomorrow.

Acknowledgements

Dedication

To my Aai,

My guru, my guide, my simple and incredibly beautiful mother.

You've always been more than a mother to me. You are my elder sister, my best friend, my world. I dedicate this book to you because you've shown me what true strength and kindness look like. You've been my inspiration at every step of the journey.

You sacrificed your dreams, your sleep, and your comfort to shape mine. It's because of your unwavering support and unconditional love that I stand where I do today. Your love kept me going. You inspired me. You healed me. You encouraged me. You made me believe.

I am a strong woman today because you raised me that way.

I hope I've made you proud.

To my Appa,

My hero, my role model.

You've raised me like a princess, and even if you don't say it out loud, I've always known how much I mean to you.

Everything you've taught me your values, your quiet strength has stayed with me. I carry them with me always, and I'll continue to live by them.

Thank you for being there, especially when I needed you the most.

Your steady energy has been my guiding force.

Appa, I may not say it often enough, but I appreciate everything you do.

You are, and always will be, the best father I could have ever wished for.

To my family

Thank you, Iyer family and Lakshmi, for believing in me and supporting me in everything I do.

Without you, none of this would be possible.

It has always been my dream to write something that could touch hearts and bring about change.

This book is just the beginning.

Thank you to everyone who has been a part of my journey.

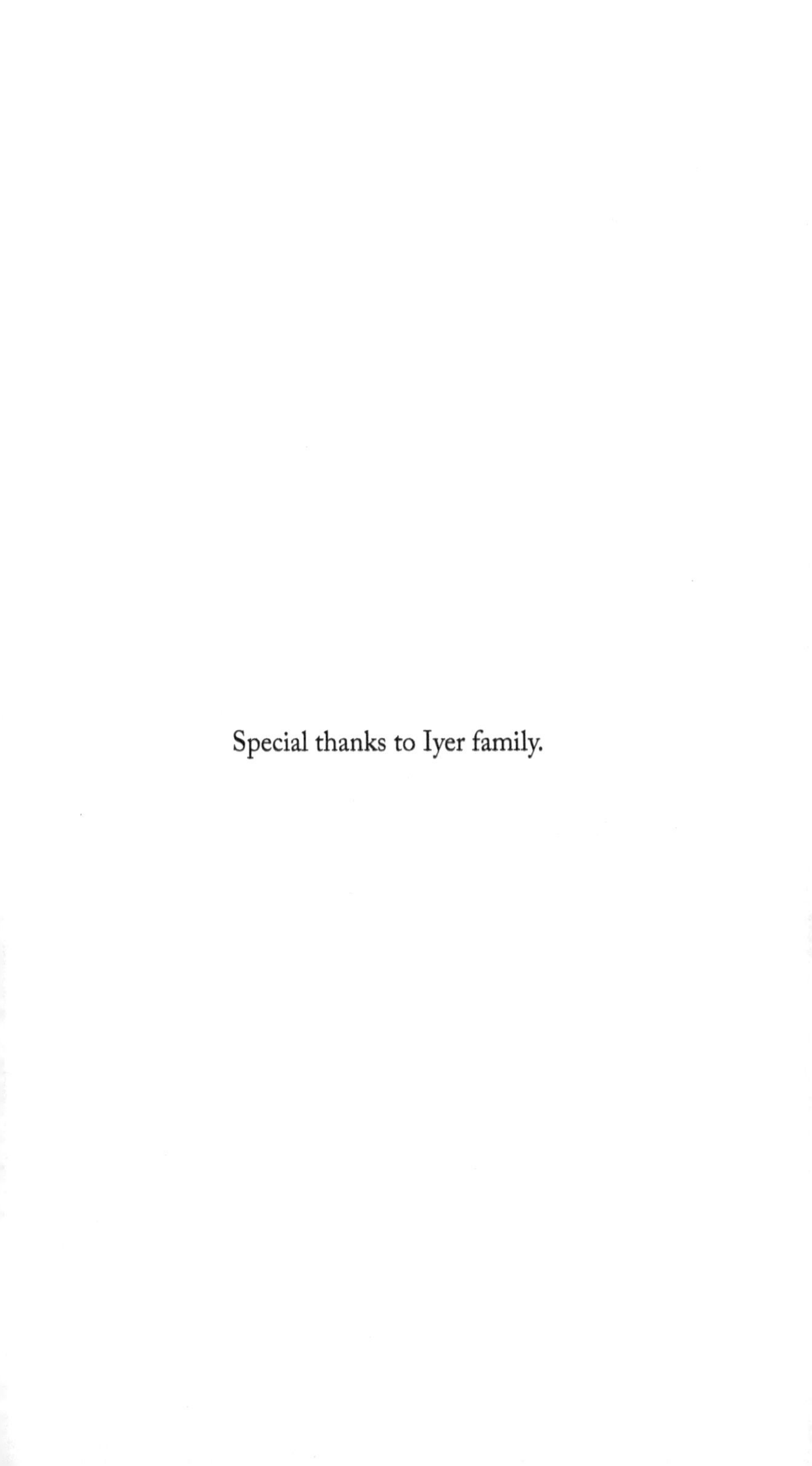

Special thanks to Iyer family.

Prologue

Let's Begin…

Do you remember your first day of college, the nervous excitement, the new faces, the dreams quietly tucked into your bag?

Do you have a best friend who knows you better than you know yourself?

Have you ever been betrayed by someone you trusted with your whole heart?

Have you ever truly fallen in love with the kind that changes you?

Do you believe in love marriage or arranged marriage? Or are you still somewhere in between?

Are your friends real, or just faces in a group photo?

Have you ever tried to give meaning to your life, beyond textbooks and timelines?

Have you ever been trapped in a relationship, unsure how to escape?

Are you the perfect child, the one who listens, obeys, and smiles even when it hurts?

Do you take care of your mother the way she once cared for you?

Have you met someone who shares your birthday and somehow feels like a mirror to your soul?

Do you think social media is safe?

Have you experienced its highs and lows, its applause and its silence?

Have you ever gone viral, even if for a moment?

If any of these questions stir something in your heart... Then this book is for you.

Because somewhere between heartbreak and healing, silence and laughter, betrayal and belonging we all search for stories that feel like our own.

Introduction to Book

"Machi Goes Viral...."

Life is not always as simple as black and white it's a spectrum of emotions, heartbreaks, laughter, friendships, and unexpected turns. *"Machi Goes Viral"* is not just a story, it's a reflection of every girl who has grown up juggling expectations, dreams, love, heartbreak, and self-discovery.

This book is a journey through the eyes of a simple, middle-class girl raised with strong values, tight family bonds, and even tighter social rules. She's someone who always followed the line but what happens when the heart starts drawing its own path?

At the core of this story is friendship: messy, beautiful, sometimes painful, but always real. *"Machi"* is not just a nickname; it's a symbol of the deepest kind of bond. But what happens when that bond is tested by love, misunderstanding, and silence?

In a world where social media becomes a stage, private moments become public, and friendships are measured in likes and comments, this is a story of a girl who accidentally goes viral, but discovers something far more important than fame.

It's about healing, owning your voice, and learning to forgive. It's about knowing when to hold on and when to let go. It's about discovering your own strength even when the world expects you to stay silent.

This book is for:

- The girl who feels torn between friendship, family and freedom.
- The best friend who didn't know how to say "I'm sorry."
- The one who fell in love when she wasn't supposed to.
- And the one who simply wants to be seen, heard, and understood.

"Machi Goes Viral" is a love letter to every emotion we've been taught to hide. It is about falling apart, finding your truth, and coming back stronger.

So, if you've ever loved deeply, lost painfully, laughed uncontrollably, or gone viral unexpectedly, this story is yours too.

MACHI GOES VIRAL…

By Shveta Iyer

Designed by Shveta Iyer

7TH JULY 2019,

Shri Krishnaswami Women's College, Anna Nagar
Chennai, {Tamil Nadu}.

"This is How, I Met Her"

7th **June 2019**, First year Bcom, Early Morning 6:30,

My Amma in between her morning prayers, {Amma in her loud voice}, Kutti ma elunthiru,elunthiru {wake up} it's 7:30 am kuttima {baby}, I woke up screaming Amma Enna? {what} ? It's 7:30 already??? Why did you wake me up so late, Amma? And I checked my phone and it was only 6:30 am, but my Amma's clock is always running one hour fast, this is how she is.

Later she was scrolling through my window curtains, my skin felt the first droplets of rain and I woke up smiling. I asked Amma, Amma raining aah? She replied', Amam heavily! She called Appa to remove the umbrellas from the Loft.

My day started with all the chaos, my mom screaming, praying loudly, appa reading the newspaper, and helping Amma with household work. but I love my family very much.

The first rain is more than just a meteorological event, it's the symbol of hope and new beginnings. It's a reminder that even in the face of adversity, nature has the power" to heal and rejuvenate. It's time for people to take a moment to appreciate the beauty of the natural world and to find solace in the simple pleasures of life, like the sound of the rain falling and the smell of the wet earth. This is truly magical and a stress breaker. Isn't it?

The sound of the rain was a symphony of nature, a rhythmic drumming against rooftops and a gentle lapping against the typical windows of South Indian houses. It was as if the entire world had tuned itself to the rain's song. Each drop that hit the earth felt like a note in a peaceful melody, washing away the exhaustion of the hot, dry days that had come before.

The air, once thick and stifling, now felt light and rejuvenating. It was cool, crisp, and carried the earthy scent of wet soil, mingled with the fragrance of blooming jasmine and the sweet smell of the rain-drenched ground. I closed my eyes, taking it all in, letting the natural perfume fill my senses, feeling the weight of the humidity lift from my body, as if the earth itself was breathing a sigh of relief.

The trees, which had been drooping under the relentless weight of the summer heat, now stood tall and proud. Their leaves glistened with raindrops, each one a tiny jewel reflecting the soft light of the overcast sky. The entire scenery transformed before my eyes what had once been dull and tired was now alive, vibrant, and full of color. The once parched earth was a lush, rich green, and every inch of nature seemed to glow with renewed energy.

I stood there for a while, feeling the cool breeze on my skin, letting the soothing sounds of the rain envelop me. It was a moment of peace, a pause in time when nature itself seemed to embrace me, offering a sense of calm, a reminder that even after the hardest of seasons, renewal would come. And with it, a new beginning just like the rain.

Heavy rains on the very first day of my college made my heart sing and dance. I was so happy to see the rain washing away the dust and the dryness that had settled over the city for far too long. It was as if the heavens themselves were celebrating with me, marking the beginning of this new chapter in my life with a grand, refreshing spectacle.

The streets were flooded in some areas, the usual chaos of traffic clogged by water blockages, but I didn't mind. Nothing could dampen my spirits that day. I could hear the rhythmic splashing of tires as vehicles made their way through the puddles, and the occasional honking seemed distant against the backdrop of the rain's soothing sound. The city felt alive, drenched in the kind of energy only the first rains could bring.

I couldn't wait to get to college, to experience everything that awaited me. The excitement was bubbling inside me new faces, new experiences, new opportunities. But above all, I was thrilled that the rainy season, my favorite of all the seasons, had decided to grace this special day.

As I walked through the waterlogged streets, my shoes splashing in the puddles, I felt free. There was something magical about the rain its power to cleanse, to refresh, and to transform even the most ordinary of days into something extraordinary. The smell of wet earth, the coolness in the air, and the soft rhythm of the rain created the perfect soundtrack for my journey into this new chapter.

I couldn't help but smile as I thought about all the memories the rainy days had given me rushing home from school in gumboots, enjoying the splash of rain on my face, the joy of jumping in puddles, and the feeling of home that only the monsoon season could bring. It was no wonder that the rainy season held such a special place in my heart. It felt like the world was giving me a little gift as I stepped into this exciting new phase of life.

Amma prepared the most delicious *adai dosa* and *filter kaapi* for me that morning. The aroma of the crispy dosas and the strong, rich smell of the freshly brewed coffee filled the house, and I couldn't help but smile. It was the perfect start to my first day of college, a comforting reminder of home before stepping into a new world.

No food in the world can beat a mother's food, because it's more than just nourishment. It's filled with emotions, love, and care. Each bite of the *adai*, with its perfect balance of spices, felt like a hug from Amma. The *filter kaapi*, with its strong yet smooth taste, brought a sense of warmth.

As I sat down to eat, I realized that no matter where life took me, no matter how many new experiences awaited, the taste of Amma's food would always ground me. It was a love language that transcended time and distance a reminder of everything she had done for me, and how much she cared.

I took my time savoring the food, each bite a little piece of home, and in that moment, I knew no matter how much I changed or how much my world shifted, the love I had for my family, and the comfort of their care, would always remain my anchor.

Wearing my favorite *kurta*, a bindi delicately placed on my forehead, oxidized jewelry that sparkled just enough to add charm, and my trusted rainy shoes this was the perfect ensemble for my first day of college. The outfit was not just about looking good, it was a reflection of my personality, a mix of tradition and modernity. Yet, there was still one last touch that was needed to make it complete.

Just as I was about to step out of the door, Amma came running behind me, her voice full of love and urgency. *"Kutti ma, wait! wait!" (oru nimisham, oru nimisham)* she called out. I turned around, and there she was, holding a small pot of *vibhuti* (sacred ash), ready to apply it on my forehead. With a smile that could light up the room, she gently pressed it onto my forehead, whispering a prayer under her breath.

It was a gesture so simple, yet so deeply meaningful. It was her way of protecting me, of sending me out into the world with her blessings and love. It was the same ritual I had seen her do for years on the first day of school, before any big event, or even when I was feeling low. This was a mother's way of reminding me that no matter where life took me, I was always under her protection, her care, and her prayers.

As I stepped closer to the door, Appa, with his deep, steady voice, stood there by the doorway, his hand resting on my shoulder. *"Good luck, kutti,"* he said, his voice filled with pride. *"May success always follow you. We are with you every step of the way."* He then showered me with his blessings, his hands raised high in a silent prayer, as if to send me off with strength and courage.

This, right here, was the essence of *Iyer Brahmin South Indian culture*, a fusion of rituals, love, and familial support that bound us all together. It wasn't just about wearing the right clothes or looking good. It was about feeling connected to something bigger, to the traditions that had been passed down through generations, and to the unconditional love of the family.

With Amma's blessings and Appa's prayers, I felt ready for whatever the day and college had to offer. And as I walked out of the house, the rain still falling softly, I couldn't help but feel grateful for the incredible foundation my family had given me.

And finally, I headed to college, my heart full of excitement, my kurta slightly damp from the misty drizzle, and in my hand, *my grandmother's very old-fashioned umbrella.*

It was one of those classic, large black umbrellas with a curved wooden handle and slightly squeaky hinges that made a faint clicking sound with every step. Most people would have found it outdated, even funny, especially with all the compact, modern umbrellas people carried around these days. But to me, it was a treasure.

This umbrella had stories, it had shielded my grandmother on temple visits, during early-morning vegetable market walks, and even accompanied her on long train journeys. Now, it was with me, on my first day of college. It felt like she was walking beside me, protecting me, blessing me in her own quiet, graceful way.

As I walked down the street, dodging puddles, splashes from passing autos, and the occasional curious glance at my "vintage" umbrella, I smiled to myself. This day was already so special not just because it was a new beginning, but because I was carrying so many pieces of my family with me.

The rain, the scent of the earth, Amma's vibhuti, Appa's blessings, and now Paati's umbrella all wrapped around me like a shield, grounding me in love, tradition, and identity.

I wasn't just stepping into college I was stepping forward with generations of strength, wrapped in the soft rhythm of rain.

Waiting at the bus stop, with raindrops trickling off Paati's umbrella and the cool breeze playing with the ends of my dupatta, I happened to glance sideways and there they were. An old couple, probably in their late seventies, stood under the narrow shade of the bus stop. Their clothes clung to them, drenched by the downpour, but their faces lit with gentle smiles told a different story. They looked like they had just returned from a temple visit. The man's forehead still had a fresh smear of vibhuti, and the lady clutched a small banana leaf packet tightly under her pallu, *likely prasadam.*

He was fussing over her in the most adorable way pulling one end of his wet *Veshtee* to gently wipe her face, trying to shield her from the remaining drops. And she, without complaining, kept swatting his hands away, while frantically tucking her purse and the sacred prasadam deeper into her sari folds, as if that was the real treasure to be protected from the rain.

They weren't speaking much, yet their silence said everything. It wasn't just shelter they were sharing, it was a lifetime. A quiet rhythm of companionship, where each movement felt rehearsed from years of caring.

Watching them, I felt something stir deep inside. It was rare to see love like that unspoken, unpolished, and beautifully ordinary. Not the kind that needed grand gestures or romantic words, but the kind that showed up in small acts… like wiping someone's face with a soaked veshtee or guarding temple prasadam like gold.

That moment, in the middle of a rainy, messy street, waiting for a bus on my first day of college, felt oddly grounding. Like a gentle whisper from the universe reminding me *this* is what matters. Love that stays. Love that serves. Love that laughs, even in the rain.

As I stood there, umbrella in one hand and college bag slung over my shoulder, I instinctively reached for my phone. The old couple drenched in rain, lost in their small world of care and quiet laughter was a perfect moment. Not posed, not staged. Just pure, raw emotion.

I'm a *street collector photographer*. Not professionally trained, but deeply observant. My passion lies in candid photography capturing stories that are happening all around us without a script. Be it street scenes, people lost in thought, dogs sleeping under old tea stalls, the chaotic beauty of the sky, or still frames of nature, my eyes are always looking for stories the world forgets to see.

I looked through the lens and gently framed the couple. I didn't want to disturb their moment; I just wanted to hold onto it. The frame had everything I loved emotion, culture, timeless love, and that soft filter of rain blurring everything just enough to make it feel like poetry. (*Click. Click.*)

One capture, and I knew this one would stay with me. Not for likes or comments but because it reminded me why I loved photography. It wasn't about aesthetics alone. It was about emotion. Truth. Connection.

My social media handle filled with skies painted by twilight, children playing with worn-out tires, temple elephants strolling calmly down narrow lanes was my personal gallery. A journal in visuals. And this picture, of a drenched elderly couple shielding love under a broken bus stop roof, was going to be a treasured addition.

I quickly edited it lightly on my phone just enhancing the contrast to bring out the shimmer of the raindrops and added it to my draft folder. Caption in my mind;

"Some love doesn't need a season. Even the rain just watches." *#streetphotography #love #candidphotography*

When my bus finally arrived, I quickly made my way inside and managed to grab my favorite window *ladies' seat.* There's something comforting about that spot, the breeze brushing my hair, the rhythmic sound of the wipers, and the world blurring outside and I drift into thoughts. It's my little moving sanctuary.

Just as I was settling in, a young woman boarded with her son, who couldn't have been more than four years old. She sat next to me, trying to calm him down as he grew increasingly restless and cranky. He kept leaning toward me, trying to wriggle out of her arms. His tiny fingers pointed eagerly at the window.

I smiled at her, and gently patted my lap, offering, *"Shall I hold him for a while?"*

She nodded with a tired but grateful smile, and soon the little one was sitting on my lap, his tiny hands pressed against the cool glass. At first, he was just curious watching the rain droplets race each other down the window. Then, slowly, that curiosity turned into laughter. He began tracing patterns on the foggy glass with his fingers, giggling every time a drop smudged his drawing.

He looked up at me once, eyes wide, and said, *"Look, aunty... rain is dancing!"* I couldn't help but laugh with him.

We sat like that for a while, me a stranger, sharing a window seat and some rain-soaked joy with a child who simply wanted to feel the world. No devices. No distractions. Just raindrops, laughter, and the hum of a moving bus.

His mother looked relieved and rested for a while. I, on the other hand, felt something more of a quiet fulfillment. That morning had already been so full of warmth and love, and here was yet another tiny reminder of life's beauty in the smallest, most unexpected places.

As the bus neared my stop, he turned and waved at me with both hands, giving me the brightest goodbye I'd had in a long time.

The joy of playing in the first rain with that little boy was nothing short of *magical*. As the rain danced on the rooftops and drummed against the pavement, it felt as though the entire world had softened its noise replaced by a melody only nature could compose.

Each *puddle* became an invitation. Each *droplet* that ran down the window was like a note in a quiet lullaby. And that boy his laughter bubbling like a stream, was the perfect companion to this fleeting moment of freedom. He wasn't just looking out of a window; he was *experiencing* the rain, one giggle at a time.

There was something about his joy that pulled me in. For a few brief minutes, I wasn't a college student worried about new beginnings or bus schedules. I was just a child again seeing the world through his eyes, rediscovering the forgotten thrill of chasing ripples and letting raindrops touch my skin without hesitation.

The smell of the wet earth, the gentle shiver in the air, the shared warmth of an umbrella, and that quiet companionship of two strangers becoming temporary friends felt like *poetry in motion*. A short story without words. A painting made only of sounds and smiles.

That moment reminded me of the *small joys* we often overlook: joys that don't come wrapped in success or achievement, but in the pure, unscripted delight of simply *being* in the moment.

As the bus rolled toward my college gates, my heart felt light, my spirit full. If the start of this new chapter had already given me such a memory, I couldn't wait to see what the rest of the day and life had in store.

As I entered through the college gate, slightly breathless but still lost in the afterglow of the rain and the boy's laughter, I paused.

The gate was beautifully decorated with handmade garlands, bright welcome banners, and colorful kolams made by the teachers themselves. Despite the heavy rains in Chennai, nothing had dampened the spirit of this place. The energy in the air felt electric buzzing with dreams, hopes, and silent introductions.

Though I was late, I didn't mind. I strolled slowly, taking in the *fresh scent of wet walls,* the chatter of students clicking selfies, and the seniors playfully guiding us towards our classes. Everything was unfamiliar, yet somehow comforting. I could already feel that this place was going to witness some of my best memories, growth, and laughter.

My heart beat a little faster not just from walking briskly but from the *exhilaration* of being part of something new. That bittersweet cocktail of *nervousness, excitement, and curiosity* swirled within me. I knew, in that moment, I was standing at the edge of something *transformative.* Not just academically but emotionally, socially, spiritually. This place was going to shape who I'd become when I finally passed out from here.

The campus buzzed with unfamiliar faces, each person with their own story, their own fears and hopes. The vibe was chaotic but warm, just like the first rain. Every step I took felt like a line in a poem I hadn't finished writing yet.

And then suddenly *"The bell rang."*

I looked down at my watch. Oh! *Fifteen minutes late.*

"Great," I muttered under my breath, clutching my bag tighter.

Without another thought, I started *running up the staircase,* my wet shoes squeaking against the marble, adrenaline kicking in. I didn't even know if I was heading in the right direction, but my legs didn't wait for my doubts to catch up.

At the top of the stairs, I could already hear *a booming voice* echoing through the corridor.

"Anirudh?"

"Present, sir!"

"Bhavana?"

"Yes, sir!"

That was definitely *Swami Mukund Sir*, famously known in campus gossip as *"Mic Mukund"* because of how loud he was even without a mic. His voice had this deep bass that could vibrate through the walls. And today, he was posted at the attendance table.

But I wasn't in the classroom yet. Because right before reaching the doorway, *bam! (chaos struck).*

Another girl, equally flustered and running with the same "I'm late and I know it" panic, collided straight into me. We both gasped as our bags slipped, and in that unfortunate instant, *our tiffin boxes flew open mid-air* like they were in a slow-motion *Kollywood* scene. Sambar, curd rice, and chutney made a modern art piece on the staircase.

"Aah! Oooh!" she winced, holding her forehead.

"Ouch, my ankle!" I winced right back, hopping on one foot.

For a moment, we both sat there messy, hurting, but strangely amused. It was the most unexpected, clumsy meet-cute of two strangers who were just trying to get through their first day.

We looked at each other, and after a pause, just burst out laughing. There was something so absurd and so *real* about the situation, it broke the ice without a word.

"I'm Vijaya," she said, still rubbing her head.

"Vellankanni," I replied, nursing my ankle.

We picked up the remains of our tiffins, exchanging embarrassed smiles and realizing our first day was off to a memorable start.

And just then, from the classroom, the voice boomed again,

"Vellankanni… Absentee!"

We scrambled to our feet and limped our way in, leaving behind not just our spilled lunch, but also the first *real* story of our college lives.

As we bent down to *gather our lunch boxes, now* cold and half-empty. I noticed something strange. I picked up a box that clearly wasn't mine, even though it *looked* exactly like it. The same stainless steel, the same way it was tied in a cloth pouch… and inside? *Idli and chutney.* Exactly what Amma had packed for me that morning.

I looked at her, and she blinked back at me. "Wait, is this yours?" She nodded slowly. "I think we switched… maybe while falling?" We both laughed, shaking our heads at our messy morning.

Once we managed to clean ourselves up as best we could wet hair, messy kurtas, dirty shoes and all we stepped into the classroom corridor. The door creaked as we opened it, and all eyes turned to us.

"Giggling. Whispering. Staring."

Everyone was clearly amused. Some were probably already cooking up nicknames or gossip. And honestly, we did look like we had just come out of a rain-themed war zone.

The professor paused mid-sentence, glanced up, and with one raised eyebrow said,

"Late. Bags down. Stand outside."

No sympathy. No lecture. Just the sentence of shame.

We nodded silently, cheeks burning, and stepped out, placing our bags at the door. We leaned against the wall, catching our breath. It was only then I absentmindedly pulled out my ID card and froze.

Wait a second.

"This isn't mine," I said, confused.

We looked at each other's IDs and suddenly, *everything stopped* for a moment.

Same blood group: O- Same birthdate: 10 August Even the same hometown.

We stared at each other, jaws slightly open. "What are the odds?" I whispered.

She laughed nervously. "Maybe… God wanted us to crash into each other. Literally."

There I was embarrassed, late to my first class, and yet… there was something oddly comforting about this. Like the universe had thrown in a little chaos to introduce me to someone who, in just an hour, already felt oddly familiar.

That was the first day I met "*Vijaya.*"

I didn't know then what role she'd play in my life or how complicated things would get in the future but at that moment, through the mess and the laughter, I felt a strange bond. It was the beginning of something. A friendship? A lesson? A destiny?

I couldn't tell. But I smiled through the mess.

Despite the chaos of our morning, something about *Vijaya* put me at ease. She had that magnetic energy loud, fearless, and totally unapologetic. I, on the other hand, was the cautious type. A bit reserved, always worried about getting into trouble. But something about her made me drop my guard.

As we stood outside the class, still technically "punished," she leaned in with a mischievous grin and whispered,

"Let's bunk the rest of this class. I'm starving. Aren't you?" I hesitated. *Bunk? On my first day? Amma would faint.*

But then, I looked at my muddy shoes, the dried raindrops on my sleeve, and her face bright, excited, already walking away. And somehow, without fully realizing it, *I followed her.*

We made our way to the college canteen, my heart pounding, Vijaya humming casually like we were just walking through a garden. The canteen had that familiar college scent *chai, fried snacks, and ink-stained benches.* Just as we approached the door, it swung open dramatically.

There stood a short, wiry man with long, wind-swept hair, holding the door like he was about to perform on a stage.

"Is your ragging done ma?" he asked in a thick local accent, mimicking Rajnikant's swagger.

Startled, I looked at Vijaya. "Uh… no?"

He smirked, flicking imaginary sunglasses from his face like the Kollywood superstar himself.

"If no ragging, then no food," he declared, stepping aside dramatically.

Vijaya burst into laughter. I didn't.

I whispered, panicked, "What does that mean? Are they serious?" She shrugged. "That's just *Kanta*, real name *Shiva*. He's been here forever. Big fan of Rajnikant. Thinks he's the principal of this canteen."

"But he just said no food!" I whispered again, a little louder this time.

"That's part of the drama, da. Come on, don't get scared."

"I am scared," I replied, clutching my dupatta like it was a shield.

Eventually, when Kanta wouldn't let us pass without the "formal ragging welcome," I pulled Vijaya aside and whispered urgently,

"Let's just go eat near the bus stop or that *Udupi* you mentioned earlier. I'm not ready for 'Rajnikant-style' college politics yet."

She sighed like I had just ruined her fun, but she agreed.

"Okay, fine," she said with a dramatic eye-roll. "But you owe me one samosa for backing out."

And just like that, we walked out of the campus gates together new

friends, hungry, slightly rebellious, but laughing. It felt like the first of many unplanned adventures.

Little did I know, this day wasn't just about *first rains or first classes* it was about the first bonds I would build, the first rules I'd quietly break, and the first steps toward discovering who I was becoming. *lol*

That day, standing near the canteen with my camera in hand, I felt completely at peace. The morning chaos had faded. I focused my lens on a *tiny nest tucked between the window grills of a mother* bird gently feeding her newborn chicks. It was such a pure sight. Life, raw and unfiltered. I clicked a few shots, adjusted the light, and thought, *This one's definitely going up on my page.* Nature always had a way of calming me.

Just as I was framing the caption for my post, I heard a loud —*dugdug-dugdug-dugdug*—the unmistakable sound of a *Royal Enfield Bullet.* Heads turned. Some even stood on their toes to peek over the crowd.

I looked up, confused.

And there she was.

Vijaya.

Riding a Bullet 350 like a total boss, one hand on the clutch, her sunglasses pushed up on her head, whistling *at me* like we were in a movie.

"MACHI va, Okar! Okaringa!" she shouted, laughing, drawing even more attention.

I couldn't help it, I just *grinned.* Something about seeing a woman confidently riding that powerful machine, in front of everyone, felt deeply empowering. And not just any woman. My new friend, my complete opposite, was causing a stir without even trying.

For a second, I saw *Appa's scooter* flash in my memory. How tightly I used to hold him, how nervous I'd be. But now, as I ran toward Vijaya's bike, hair flying, dupatta clutched in one hand, I felt… free.

This was the first time I ever sat behind someone other than Appa, and I wasn't afraid. I was excited.

Everyone around stared at students clicking pictures, murmuring things, and even some professors shaking their heads, amused or mildly annoyed. But we didn't care.

We zoomed out of campus, the wind drying off the last bit of rain from our clothes. After a bit of a search through narrow lanes and side roads, we found a *small Udupi restaurant* tucked away between a Xerox shop and a flower stall. The aroma of fresh sambar hit us before we even stepped in.

Sliding into a steel-framed booth, she looked at me with a smirk, "So, how much cash?"

"Only ₹50," I said nervously.

"Perfect," she grinned. "I've got ₹40."

With ₹90 between us, we ordered one *crispy dosa* and *two filter coffees,* split perfectly. While we waited, I sat there silently watching her.

Let me tell you, Vijaya wasn't just a personality, she was a *storm.*

Short in height, bold boy-cut hair dyed copper red, a little flirty, definitely mischievous, and dressed in rugged jeans with a graphic tee that read *"Rebel with a cause."*

She had 368k followers on social media. A local celeb. And me? I was her opposite.

I am selectively social,

Long hair, soft voice, careful words.

I was introverted, loved my journals, cameras, and peaceful skies. She loved reels, bikes, and making noise.

But sitting across from her, laughing over a shared dosa, I realized something:

Perfect friendship isn't about similarity. It's about balance.

It's when two opposites come together, not to change each other, but to add color, chaos, and calm in just the right amounts.

And in that tiny Udupi café, with the clink of coffee tumblers and the smell of masala dosa in the air, a quiet bond began to form one I didn't know would later change my life in unexpected ways.

The bus ride back home was a blend of exhaustion and excitement. My mind replayed the entire day, starting from the chaos of the first rain, meeting "Vijaya", the awkwardness of the ID mix-up, and the unexpected bond we had formed. As the bus swayed with the rhythm of the traffic, I couldn't help but smile at the thought of her—her confidence, her carefree attitude, and the way she turned every little moment into something memorable.

We had barely known each other for a few hours, but it felt like I had known her for years. The way she wasn't afraid to speak her mind, the way she effortlessly brightened the dullest moments, made me think I had truly met someone special.

When I reached home, I couldn't wait to talk to "*Kalyani*", my younger sister. She always had a knack for listening and understanding, no matter how silly the stories were.

I rushed into the living room, where Kalyani was lounging on the couch, scrolling through her phone. Her eyes sparkled when she saw my excited face.

"What happened, did you have a good day?" she asked with a teasing smile.

I plopped down next to her, sharing everything, the rain, the crash on the staircase, the chocolate, and the quirky girl who had become my unexpected companion for the day.

Kalyani listened intently, her eyes wide with curiosity. "Wait... so you're telling me you've already found a friend like that? On your first day? And you both are completely different from each other?"

"Yeah," I said, laughing. "It feels strange but... right. She's everything I'm not, and yet, we just clicked."

Kalyani nodded thoughtfully. "That's actually so cool, *akka*. It's like you guys balance each other out."

I couldn't have said it better myself.

Later that evening, after dinner, I couldn't help but think about how *different* everything had felt. The whole day, though chaotic and imperfect, was now a beautiful memory in my heart. Vijaya, with her wild energy, her fierce independence, and her ability to turn any awkward moment into a funny one, had already made such a big impact on me.

As I lay in bed that night, I thought about what she said to me earlier: *"Sometimes, it's okay not to be okay."*

In that moment, I understood it wasn't just a casual saying. It was her way of reminding me that it was okay to be imperfect. That sometimes, life doesn't go as planned, and that's completely okay.

I had never thought about things this way, but Vijaya, the girl who was a complete contrast to me in so many ways, had somehow shown me a new perspective. Life was about learning from those moments, not being afraid of them.

And so, as I closed my eyes that night, I felt a strange calmness wash over me. Tomorrow was a new day, and I was ready for whatever it would bring.

"Entirely Different Worlds"

My second day of college felt like the world had finally settled into place. The nervousness had melted into excitement, and the unfamiliar faces started looking a little more familiar. And the biggest reason for this comfort?

was "Vijaya."

We now shared a bench in every class. She called it "our spot." She'd always drop her bag with a dramatic *thud* on the bench before plopping down next to me like it was her throne. I would quietly unpack my books while she'd start a casual conversation with the entire row, waving at classmates like a local celebrity which, let's be honest, she sort of was.

Though we came from *entirely different worlds*, there was an unspoken ease between us.

I stayed with my parents and younger sister, Kalyani, in a peaceful home where mornings started with Amma's prayers and Appa's newspaper rustling.

Vijaya, on the other hand, lived in a *PG (paying guest accommodation)*, cooked instant noodles when she was late, and handled everything on her own.

She was the only child of her parents, and though she never said it out loud, I could feel a sense of quiet loneliness tucked beneath her loud laughter. Maybe that's why she clung to the people she liked so fiercely because deep down, she didn't want to feel alone.

During breaks, we'd sit under the neem tree near the canteen, sharing food and stories. She'd always steal the best part of my lunch, *the medu-vada*, every time and I'd pretend to be annoyed. But honestly, I didn't mind. In return, she'd offer me half her *veg-milk cake or a slice of chocolate she always kept in her bag "for sad days." lol-*

She began opening up slowly, telling me about her parents who stayed in Madurai, her mom who was overprotective, and how she missed home-cooked food but didn't like to admit it. I would often pack an extra idli or two for her, and she'd pretend like she was just *"tasting"* it.

What surprised both of us was how easily we *fit into each other's worlds.* She taught me how to let go a little, how to take spontaneous bike rides after college, and how to enjoy the moment without always planning the next step.

And I, in turn, taught her how to slow down, to find comfort in the calm, and how sometimes, quiet companionship could say more than a hundred words.

We were *opposites* in background, in behavior, even in fashion. But in some strange way, we were exactly what the other needed.

And over the weeks, that bond *from strangers, to friends, to best buddies* became the most precious part of my college life.

THIS CHAPTER IS *GOLDEN!*

After a month 7th July 2019, will forever be stamped in my heart like a warm melody.

From the minute I woke up, I could feel the tension in my chest, but also a strange sense of hope. *Election result day*, not for politics, but for something that mattered way more to me, the inter-college singing competition.

I still remember Amma's voice from the kitchen, humming one of our bhajan tunes as she made filter coffee. Amma wasn't just my mom, she was my *guru*, my first musical cheerleader, and every Sunday we sang together, just the two of us, in our little temple corner. She had been training me since I was four, and this competition meant everything to both of us.

My palms were sweating as I reached college, but Vijaya? She was already bouncing near the notice board like a squirrel who had eaten too much sugar. Her eyes scanned the sheet like she was decoding a mission briefing.

Then she screamed my name.

"Vellankanni! Vellankanni! You are selected!"

I didn't even check the list. I just ran to her and hugged her tightly. We both jumped like kids who had won a school picnic trip. The moment felt magical.

I dialed Amma.

"Ammaaaa… I got selected!"

Her voice broke on the other end with happiness. "Paavam, I told you! My kutti singer is going to shine!"

I was the only girl selected from "Krishna Swami College," and I could feel the weight of pride and responsibility settling on my shoulders. But Vijaya was having none of that seriousness.

"Machi vaango, sit on bike," she said in her usual bossy tone. "Today, *we* should celebrate!"

We headed out and gobbled spicy street-side *mirchi bhajji* with tea so strong it could revive a dead phone battery. The rains didn't stop though and like a classic Chennai afternoon, it came down hard.

By 2 pm, I got a call from my professor.

"Vellankanni, go to "Anna Adarsh College" and complete the competition formalities."

I looked at Vijaya. She was already starting her bike.

"Ride ready," she smirked. "Let's go Machi, My superstar."

Now here's the thing: "Anna Adarsh" was known as a *boy's college*, and walking in drenched and messy was *NOT* how I planned to make my first impression. But fate doesn't care about your hair or your shoes.

The Singing room was pin-drop silent. Only the *squelch squelch* sound of our *wet shoes* echoed in that overly clean room. The minute we stepped inside

"*Aiyo! You both wait outside!*" the teacher snapped.

"Our floors are not swimming pools!"

I could feel my stomach twist. *Was this it? Was I going to get disqualified because monsoon fashion fails?*

I whispered, "Vijaya, what now?"

But she, unfazed as ever, leaned against the wall and casually scanned the corridor.

"*Machi… I'm in love.*" she whispered dramatically.

"*What??*" I said, my eyebrows jumping halfway to my hairline. "With *whom*? What love? What drama?"

"That boy… that one…" she said, subtly pointing with her eyes.

I turned. There he was. A guy draped in a *bright green saree*, running toward the washroom. He had long lashes, a mischievous grin, and a spark in his eyes.

"They're probably having some fancy dress or cultural round," Vijaya whispered like she was narrating a crime scene.

"When I say 'parr parr', turn, okay?"

Moments later, as predicted, the green-saree boy came out adjusting his pallu like he had walked out of a movie set. **"Parr parr!"** Vijaya whispered.

I turned my head and bam, our eyes met.

He was already looking at us.

I quickly turned back, cheeks flushing, and looked at her. *"Woohoo… good choice machi."*

We both burst out laughing, trying to cover our faces like two teenagers caught spying.

That day, everything from the joy of selection, to the rain, to Vijaya's impromptu crush on a boy in a saree, felt like a scene from one of those heartwarming coming-of-age movies. A story about dreams, friendships, and the unpredictable magic of ordinary days.

And as we stood outside that room, with soaked shoes and soaked hearts, I realized *"these are the days we'll remember forever."*

After the formalities were done, we stepped out of the staffroom, our shoes still leaving wet traces on the staircase. I was more focused on not slipping, but Vijaya? She had radar locked on only one thing—*Siddharth Madhavanan.*

The moment we reached the bottom of the steps, she bumped into someone and squealed, *"Vasu daa!"*

It was her old school friend. They hugged, laughed, and quickly got into that fast-paced Tamil catch-up mode. While she was chatting away with Vasu, my eyes completely drifted toward the college gate.

There he was.

"Siddharth."

Now surrounded by a bunch of other guys, *all* in sarees, laughing, taking selfies, full-on energy.

But the strange part?

He was looking straight at me.

Not blinking. Just *looking*.

I froze. Looked away quickly. Then again… peeked through the corner of my eye.

What was this? Was I overthinking?

My mind was racing faster than the Chennai metro.

Before I could figure anything out, *Vijaya had already gotten all the details.*

She turned to me with stars in her eyes.

"Machi, his name is Siddharth Madhavanan! GR of the college. Million followers on social media. Content creator. Animal lover. Bullet lover. Activist. LOOK AT HIM, **Oh wow ! How wow he is machi"**

She was already stalking his profile.

"Idha paaru da! Look at this post—feeding stray dogs. This one rally for water rights. This one him doing yoga on a mountain! He's my dream guy. I swear."

I laughed, "Okay okay, calm down. He doesn't even know your name yet!"

"No no no… He will. And I will flaunt *full-a full-a*. Wait and watch, Machi."

She asked me to wait near the gate while she zoomed into the parking area.

And guess what?

Within a few minutes, she came back with her *Bullet 350*, looking like a Kollywood superstar. Helmet hanging on one handle, hair slightly flying in the breeze, eyes sparkling with madness.

People turned. Boys stared. Professors peeked.

And me? I quickly covered my face with a scarf like some filmi heroine trying to escape paparazzi. *Lol*

She tossed me the helmet. *"Va da! Let's give them a show."*

And *zoom*, we rode off.

The engine roared. Rain droplets hit us like tiny needles. And Vijaya? She had this huge grin plastered on her face and didn't stop talking about *Siddharth* the entire way back.

"I think he's the one. I can feel it. I just got over two horrible breakups da. This feels different. I don't know, but… I want to try again."

I nodded, quietly listening. She had been through a lot in the past few weeks—*heartbreak, trust issues, pain* she didn't talk about much. So seeing her this excited again? Seeing her hopeful?

"It made me happy."

Even if it was just a crush or the beginning of something real, her energy was contagious.

As she rode on, her voice mixed with the sound of rain and the hum of the Bullet, I smiled behind the helmet.

Somewhere deep inside, I knew this day was going to be golden, *a turning point.*

"The Night of the Finale."

July-2019,

The hall was glowing under golden lights, and the air buzzed with excitement and tension. Backstage, my palms were cold, my throat dry, my mind running in loops. This wasn't just any performance. It was *the* performance I had imagined since I was a little girl.

A dream I had woven quietly in my room.

A dream Amma had nurtured with her soft *taans* during evening bhajans. A dream I had whispered into the corners of my notebook while doodling musical notes in class.

The moment finally arrived.

They called my name. "Vellankanni"

I stood up. My legs felt heavy, but my heart was racing. I walked to the stage, the spotlight now burning on me like the sun after a long eclipse. I couldn't look at the crowd. So I found the one anchor I trusted, *Vijaya.*

She was sitting in the second row, eyes locked onto mine, giving me that "you've got this" nod. That's all I needed.

I closed my eyes. Took a deep breath.

Let the music guide you, I told myself. *This is your moment.*

And I sang.

Every note was drenched in emotion. Every line carried my story. Every pause was a prayer. I forgot about the judges. I forgot about the crowd. For those three minutes, it was just me and the music.

And when I ended, there was silence… then an explosion of cheers. Claps. Whistles. The crowd was on its feet.

I opened my eyes, tears glistening, and the first person I saw was *Vijaya,* clapping so hard like she was going to fly. Her eyes were watery too.

She mouthed,

"Machi, you did it."

A few moments later, the results were announced.

"And the winner of the inter-college singing competition is… Vellankanni from Krishna Swami College!"

My knees went weak. I froze for a second. Then Vijaya grabbed my hand, pulling me up.

"You've flown, da. You *finally* flew."

That moment was not just about winning a trophy.

It was about proving to myself that I *could.*

That little girl with dreams wasn't little anymore. She had *arrived.*

That night, we celebrated like never before.

Rain, street lights, a shared dosa at a roadside shop, and one filter coffee with extra sugar.

We laughed, we clicked silly selfies, and I knew… this was just the *"**beginning.**"*

"Victory Week Was in Full Swing."

Posters with my face were pinned across campus boards, corridors, and even the canteen walls. Some carried my solo photo holding the trophy, others had me mid-performance with my eyes closed and mouth wide open in a high note. It felt surreal. But the most *unexpected* surprise?

was "Vijaya."

She arrived in college riding her Bullet like a superstar, with a *custom-made flag* of my poster fluttering behind her.

"Machi-The Superstar singer, Vellankanni!" she screamed, parking dramatically in front of the library.

Everyone clapped and laughed.

I was embarrassed, but my heart was glowing. She was truly proud of me.

That afternoon, around 2, while we were sitting on the stone bench near the peepal tree, Vijaya leaned in.

"Machi…" she said softly, "the competition is over… but I'm still stuck. I miss *him* da."

I already knew who she meant.

She didn't even have to say his name anymore.

"Siddharth?" I asked, raising my eyebrow.

She nodded, her face half-serious, half-dreamy.

"Let's just go see him once no? *Just one look*, during lunch break. What do you say? Please please do me this favor."

I rolled my eyes, "No way. I'm tired. And I promised Appa I've go home early today."

But Vijaya had a superpower—*convincing me*.

She pressed her palms together like a dramatic heroine from an old Tamil movie, "I swear, fifteen minutes only! We go, we see, we zoom back. Promise. Plus, Bullet ride too!"

I sighed, smiled, and finally agreed.

As we rode through the slightly flooded Chennai streets, she asked, "Why don't you like Siddharth da? Like not even a little?"

I paused.

It wasn't about liking or not liking. It was about *survival*.

"My parents are very strict, machi. Even if I *ever* liked someone, they'd... kill me, throw me out maybe. So I've shut those doors. Locked them permanently."

She didn't say anything for a moment.

Then softly, she said, "I don't know if I'm serious about him. But the way he speaks… his ideas, his presence… *something* makes my heart race."

We finally reached *Anna Adarsh College*, expecting to just sneak a glance.

But something was different today.

Outside the campus, a small group of students stood with placards, shouting slogans. There was a buzz in the air.

"We Demand Change!" "Stop Misuse of Power!" "Voices Will Be Heard!"

We stood there confused. That's when we saw him.

Siddharth.

At the center of it all, holding a banner high above his head:

"WE DEMAND CHANGE."

His expression was calm, but his eyes were fierce. Focused.

Vijaya froze next to me. Her words were a whisper.

"Machi… he's not just handsome… he's fearless too."

Back at college, Vijaya was glowing.

She parked the Bullet, tossed off her helmet like a scene straight out of a movie, and smiled at me like a kid who had just won a prize.

"Machi! He followed me! He followed me!" She was practically dancing on the pavement.

I smiled, trying to be happy for her. But my mind was somewhere else Siddharth's gaze, the urgency in his footsteps, the way he looked straight at me through the window before everything turned chaotic.

Was he really coming down just for us? Or was it... for *me?*

But before I could figure anything out, boom. Another twist.

Later that evening, as I was washing dishes with Amma humming bhajans in the background, my phone buzzed. A *friend request.*

From *Siddharth Madhavanan.*

My hand paused midway over a soapy glass.

I wiped my fingers, picked up the phone, and stared.

Why me?

It didn't make sense. He followed *Vijaya* first, the one with the helmet ID, the one who liked him, the one who had that spark in her eyes since day one. So... why now *me?*

Was it just a polite gesture? Random? A mistake?

Or... was he trying to say something?

I opened his profile, carefully scrolling.

Pictures of college protests, animal rescues, his dog "Chinna", quotes about justice, rain-soaked roads, temple bells, chai cups, bullet rides…

He wasn't just handsome — he was grounded. He stood for something. And that was rare.

But still, I didn't accept.

Not because I wasn't curious… but because I was scared.

Scared of misunderstandings. Scared of hurting Vijaya. And honestly? Scared of *what this might become.*

So I kept quiet.

Didn't tell her. Didn't respond.

But my heart knew, something was shifting. And I'd have to face it, sooner or later. (completely my instinct or assumptions)

"Seeing a Rainbow for the First Time."

Next Day – 8:30 AM, Shri Krishnaswami College,

I was already in class, seated near the window, pretending to read my notes. But honestly? I was just waiting for her.

Vijaya walked in like she owned the campus hair bouncing, wearing a fresh tee, and flaunting a *brand new headset.* She was glowing, absolutely glowing.

I, on the other hand, was *fuming.*

I didn't even wait for her to sit down.

"Enna da machi? Where were you last night? I called you so many times, messaged you! I was worried!"

She laughed. Not even a guilty laugh, a full-blown *"Uff machi!"*

And then casually said,

"I was busy following and liking all of his pictures! Time just flew… forgot to even charge my phone!"

That was it. I could feel my cheeks getting hot.

Here I was, worried sick that maybe she was upset, or something went wrong… and she? She was having a social media romance with

Siddharth's profile.

Before I could say anything else, she leaned over, kissed my cheek, and hugged me tight.

"Sowwy da kutti. Don't be mad. I'm just really happy, okay? It's been so long since I felt this spark. He's different. I feel seen, you know?"

I sighed. I couldn't stay angry. Not with her.

She was smiling like a child seeing a rainbow for the first time. And I remembered her breakdowns. The tears after those breakups. The way she curled up on my lap saying no one would ever love her truly.

So I nodded.

"Okay da… but please, just slow down a bit. Not everyone is as genuine as they look on social media. I don't want you hurt again."

She tapped my forehead playfully.

"That's why I have you, my filter. If anything goes wrong, you'll catch it first. Deal?"

And with that, we went back to being *us*. The chaos, the teasing, the bond.

"A Shadow in the Back of My Mind."

S ame Day – Around 2:00 PM,

I was standing near the college gate, waiting for Vijaya to come out of the restroom. That's when I noticed two guys on bikes, parked just across the street.

One of them… I recognized.

Anna Adarsh College. Siddharth's circle. I'd seen him with him before.

At first, I thought it was just a coincidence. But then they approached.

"Hey… mind sharing your number? Just want to be friends." The way they smiled… it wasn't friendly. It felt invasive. Cold.

I didn't respond , just gave them the *deadliest* stare I could manage. My heart was pounding, but I stood my ground.

They smirked, muttered something to each other, and left.

The moment Vijaya came out, I told her everything.

"Machi, two guys just came and asked for my number. One of them I've seen with Siddharth. I don't know if he sent them or I don't want to assume but it just felt… off."

She paused, then took a deep breath.

"Ignore da. Don't let random boys shake your day. Maybe they're just being jobless fellows. Siddharth wouldn't do that. Don't overthink it."

Maybe she was right. Maybe I was overreacting. But something in me… didn't sit well.

Later that evening, we both attended the concert event organized by our college. It was held at a nearby college ground. The music, the crowd, the chaos, it was the perfect escape. Vijaya danced her heart out, and for a while, even I forgot the unease. We clicked selfies, cheered for our college bands, and soaked in the night's rhythm. Vijaya gone live on her social media channel.

But somewhere deep down, I knew that moment at the gate wasn't over. It had left a *mark* a shadow in the back of my mind.

"Our Day, Our Birthday Da Machi."

August 10, 2019

A few weeks had passed, and suddenly it was *our* day — *our birthday.*

Yes! *Vijaya and I shared the same birthday, and same blood group O-.* A coincidence? Maybe. But to me, it was fate, like the universe knew we were meant to find each other in this lifetime.

That morning, at exactly 7:00, Amma entered my room, quietly drawing back my window curtains. The soft drizzle had painted the sky in a dreamy gray. She leaned in and whispered,

"Endra endra kutti ma… Happy birthday, kuttima."

Her voice was warm and filled with love. That gentle wish, right into my ear, wrapped me in comfort. I woke up smiling, my heart already full.

She handed me a small, beautifully wrapped gift, a baby pink kurti, perfectly my style and tucked a crisp *₹500 note* inside with it.

"For your birthday cravings," she smiled.

That moment her thoughtful touch, the gift, her effort to make me feel loved made my birthday morning extra special.

Next to me, Kalyani, still curled up in her blanket, mumbled in her sleepy voice,

"Happy birthday akka..."

I laughed softly, hugged her tightly, and stayed like that for a few more minutes soaking it all in.

Then, my phone buzzed. A notification.

"Happy Birthday to both of us, darling! Machi, I love you!" It was *Vijaya*. My day just lit up even more.

I replied immediately,

"Machi, I love you too, to the moon and back! Happy birthday to you too! See you soon in college!"

Down at the breakfast table, Amma had gone all out for a special birthday breakfast just for me. She had cancelled her usual errands just to spend this time with me. From soft idlis to hot kesari and coffee, every bite was her way of saying "I love you."

Wearing my brand-new baby pink kurti, I touched Appa and Amma's feet, received their blessings, and left home with a huge smile.

As I reached the bus stop, I heard the familiar *dug-dug-dug* of a Bullet. I looked up, and there she was *Vijaya*. Dressed in a sharp new tee and denim, she looked more confident than ever.

I screamed,

"Machi, Happy Birthday! I love you! Thank you for the surprise!"

She smiled wide and said,

"Anything for you, machi!"

We zoomed through the city's morning drizzle, birthday twins on a mission.

At college, the vibe was different. Word had spread, and everyone was wishing us. We exchanged gifts, I gave her a stylish handbag and she gifted me a beautiful pen set.

Small, thoughtful gestures that meant everything.

Vasu, her friend, joined us for lunch, and the three of us had a blast. Laughter, selfies, fun all of it was captured in pictures. Vijaya, without missing a beat, posted our snaps on social media and tagged me with a cute caption.

Soon, her riding group, friends, and followers began pouring in wishes, love, and comments.

The response was overwhelming people from across her social circles shared the joy of our bond.

That's when I realized:

Sometimes, social media can be a beautiful space when used right to spread kindness, love, and connection. It amplified the joy we already had.

Late evening, at 8:30, Amma had cooked a warm, hearty dinner full of my favorites. We all sat together, laughing, eating, and wrapping up the perfect birthday.

And I knew — *this birthday would stay etched in my heart forever.*

"A Month Later – New Turns."

It had been a month since our birthday, time was moving fast, and so were the quiet undercurrents in our lives.

By now, *Vijaya and Siddharth* had become social media friends. But they hadn't exchanged numbers yet.

I actually found comfort in that they were taking things slow, allowing space for a bond to grow without rushing into anything. And for once, I was relieved.

Lunch Break — Around 2 PM | Canteen

I was in the canteen, surrounded by friends, caught up in a lively game of Antakshari. Laughter filled the space as voices echoed old Hindi and Tamil melodies.

Vijaya walked in — glowing.

She looked... different. Happy, but a little tense. Like her heart was full of fluttering butterflies.

She sat beside me and whispered, *"Machi... I got a message from Siddharth!"* I paused the game, eyes wide.

"WHAT? Seriously?"

She nodded, her cheeks flushed pink.

She showed me the message:

"Hi, Siddharth Madhavanan this side. Would you love to meet me?

Maybe after college?"

Just that. Simple. Direct. Brave.

I looked at her face, beaming with *nervous excitement.*

Siddharth had finally made a move and it was no longer just 'likes' and DMs.

It was real.

I told her, softly,

"You're free to do what feels right, machi. Go meet him. Explore. But…" She raised her eyebrows.

"But?"

"…Today's Kalyani's birthday. We're all going out for dinner, so I need to head home early."

She nodded, understanding.

"No problem. And yes, I'll be careful. I promise. Just pray he doesn't turn out to be another clown like the last two!" We both laughed.

Before I left, I looked at her, my heart swelling with care.

"Hey… whatever happens, promise me you'll stay safe, hmm?"

She kissed my forehead and said,

"Yes, machi. Sure I will. And I'll tell you everything later."

I boarded the bus, window seat as always, and let the city drift past me.

My phone buzzed with birthday wishes for *Kalyani*.

As I sat there, I couldn't help but smile as life was slowly weaving its patterns. Friendships, love, family, dreams. All unfolding at their own pace.

That evening, I was heading toward home, toward family, toward celebration.

But my thoughts stayed with *Vijaya and her new chapter.*

"Evening of Reflections"

*K*alyani Turns 18,

Evening at 8:30, our home was wrapped in warmth.

Amma was glowing with joy when her youngest, Kalyani, had turned eighteen.

The dinner table buzzed with laughter, clinking cutlery, and delicious smells of Amma's finest dishes.

It was a night of celebration, of family, of memories.

But somewhere in the middle of all the joy, the air shifted.

Appa cleared his throat.

The room went quiet, and he looked at me with a calm but serious expression.

"So... we've started thinking,"

"It's time we start looking for a good match for you."

My heart skipped a beat.

"The laughter faded inside me."

Of course, I knew this moment would come. But not tonight. Not so soon.

I tried to smile, but my fingers were clenched under the table.

"Appa, please... let me finish my final exams first," I said softly.

He chuckled, kindly.

"Yes, yes! I'm not rushing anything. We'll align this *after* your Third Year exams. Don't worry."

I nodded, grateful — at least that gave me some breathing room.

Later, in the car, things got more *intense.*

Amma, seated beside me, was whispering Her voice filled with concern, not anger.

"Vellankanni... tell me honestly... is there *someone* you like?"

My chest tightened.

"No Amma! There's no one..."

She looked at me long and hard.

"You know Appa will not be okay with any love marriage. You know how it is."

"Just remember, our family won't allow such things. Not for you. Not for Kalyani either."

There it was *clear, direct, traditional.*

I nodded again. Not because I fully agreed but because I understood. These were not just their expectations, these were their values. Their identity.

And in a way, mine too.

I told them, gently:

"Amma, Appa... I will follow your wishes. I respect your decision."

"But please... let me first finish my studies. Let me give my First year exams with a clear mind."

That night, *my words seemed to reach them. Appa placed a hand on my head* and said:

"That's my girl. Mature and understanding."

And Amma smiled, her eyes moist with both pride and relief.

Even though the weight of expectations sat quietly on my shoulders,

I felt proud — because I stood my ground without breaking their trust.

I realized, growing up isn't just about choices.

It's about balancing dreams and duties.

About finding peace between who you are and who you're expected to be.

And that night, as the city lights blinked past the car window, I whispered a silent prayer:

Let me do justice to both, my dreams and their hopes.

"The Breaking Point."

8:30 AM – Bus Stop

Vijaya was already waiting for me.

But something was different today.

She wasn't her usual vibrant, loud self.

She looked... numb. Sad. Distant. Her eyes gave away something that her lips weren't ready to say.

"Machi, are you okay?"

"What's wrong?"

She didn't answer right away. She barely looked at me.

"I'll tell you during the lunch break," she said quietly.

1:00 PM – College Canteen

We sat down. I was nervous, my heart pounding, not knowing what to expect.

And then Vijaya spoke.

"Machi... I need to tell you something important."

"I met Siddharth yesterday. At a coffee shop. With one of his friends."

I blinked, not understanding where this was going.

"He… he confessed his feelings for you Vellu. He likes you. A lot."

My heart stopped for a second.

"What?"

"What nonsense are you talking about?"

But Vijaya was serious. She held my hand and said it again, slower this time:

"He told me. He likes you, not me."

I was flooded with confusion, disbelief, and a strange sense of betrayal. Was this some kind of prank?

"Vijaya, stop it. This isn't funny."

"He liked *you*. You liked *him*. Why are you dragging me into this Vijaya?"

She shook her head, calmly but firmly.

"No machi, that was our assumption. I was never in the picture. He's always had eyes for you."

"I know what I felt before, but I've seen enough people to know when someone is being genuine."

I didn't know how to process this.

Just last night, my Appa had told me he'd begun searching for a groom. That conversation was still echoing in my head.

"Vijaya, no! This... this can't happen."

"My family would never allow it. I *can't* go against them."

She tried to reason with me. She called Siddharth a good man. Said I should at least consider his feelings. Just meet him once.

But I snapped.

"Vijaya,

I said no!" "I'm not like you. I'm from a middle-class family. I live with rules. I can't dream about some random boy just because he rides a Bullet and has followers!"

She was still insisting.

She held my hand too tightly.

Something inside me broke.

I stood up... and slapped her.

Right there.

In front of the entire canteen.

Everything went silent.

Vijaya's face turned pale. Her eyes didn't tear up. But the hurt the disbelief was crystal clear.

She didn't say a word.

She simply picked up her bag and walked out of the campus.

That Evening,

The silence was heavier than usual at home.

Amma kept staring at me.

"What's wrong, kutti?" she asked.

"You're not yourself."

I forced a smile and shook my head.

"Nothing Amma… just tired. Assignments. Exams…"

But deep down, I was aching.

I couldn't stop thinking about what had happened.

How fast things spiraled. How one friendship, once full of laughter and dreams, now stood broken because of a moment of anger and confusion.

I didn't know how to fix it. Or even if it could be fixed.

Amma was feeling everything.

And no matter how close you are to your mother… Sometimes, it's the deepest feelings you can't share.

Same Night – 9:30,

Later that night, Amma wasn't feeling well.

She had acidity and a mild fever. She looked weak and tired, yet she was still walking around, trying to finish her chores.

I gently held her hand and said,

"Amma, please sit. I'll take care of the rest."

She gave me a tired smile, trying to hide her discomfort, but I could see through it.

Watching her like that tugged at my heart.

That's when I made a decision I'd stay home tomorrow.

I needed to take care of her.

But honestly, I also needed to breathe. To pause.

The conflict with Vijaya had left me shaken.

And college suddenly felt like a place I didn't want to step into, at least not for a day.

Maybe the silence at home would help me process what had happened.

Maybe Amma's presence would calm the storm inside me.

I sat beside her that night, helped her eat a few spoons of rice, gave her her medicine, and tucked her into bed.

She whispered,

"You're my strength, kutti."

And I realized this is my world. My Amma, Appa, and Kalyani.

They may have strict rules. They may not understand everything. But their love was unconditional.

That night, I lay awake staring at the ceiling, not thinking of Siddharth. Not even Vijaya.

Just Amma.

And how sometimes, being there for the people who've always been there for you is all the healing you really need.

"A House Full of Quiet Storms."

The Next Morning, at 8.

I woke up late.

Even though Amma was still unwell, I found her in the kitchen, moving around slowly, trying to prepare breakfast.

I rushed in, gently held her shoulders and said,

"Amma, please rest… I'll make the coffee today."

She resisted at first but eventually sat down with a tired nod.

I brewed two cups, strong and sweet, just the way she liked.

Appa joined us soon after, holding two photographs in his hand.

I knew what they were before he even spoke. Appa was taking his search for a groom seriously now.

He didn't say much. Just placed the photos on the table and gave Amma a knowing glance.

Despite all the emotional noise inside me, I remained silent.

Maybe it was easier to not speak than to say something that would disappoint them.

Later, Amma walked into my room with the same photos.

She sat beside me, quietly handed them over, and waited.

I looked at them… but not really.

I wasn't ready for this. Not yet. Not now.

"A Buzz I Didn't Expect."

L unch Hour, 12:30

I placed my phone on charge and sat with my family for lunch. Within moments, my phone started *buzzing continuously.*

Kalyani noticed first.

"Akka, your phone's gone crazy…check! So many notifications!"

Appa shot me a sharp look. Not angry exactly, just intense. But I couldn't understand what I had done.

I barely use social media that much… so why this sudden flood?

Curious and a little nervous, I picked it up.

And there it was *message after message* from *Raja,* Siddharth's friend. He had texted me *"Hi" five times.*

Just "Hi."

But in that moment, it felt loud. Intrusive. Unwelcome.

I hadn't spoken to him before. He didn't have a reason to text me. Not after what had happened with *Vijaya.* Not now.

I didn't even think. I just blocked him.

It was a reflex maybe anger, maybe discomfort, maybe my way of saying,

"Please, not again."

"Back to What Matters."

A mma and Exams,

Amma still wasn't feeling great.

So I decided not to return to college that day.

I told myself I'd stay home, study, and be there for her.

Maybe focusing on my books would help me silence the noise in my head.

Maybe being near Amma would help me heal, too.

Between preparing for finals and watching over her, I felt like I was balancing two worlds

One built on expectations, the other built on care.

And somewhere between the two, I was trying not to fall apart.

"The Eye Contact That Said Everything."

After weeks away from college, I finally returned. The air felt different.

Not because of the exam pressure but because *she* was there.

Vijaya.

We hadn't spoken since that day in the canteen.

But when our eyes met across the classroom,

it wasn't anger or coldness we exchanged… it was something softer distant, but knowing.

A silent glance.

As if both of us, despite everything, still remembered what we once were.

"The Door We Never Opened."

After the Exam,

Once the exam ended, I headed to the canteen to collect some change from Kanta.

And there she was Vijaya standing at the canteen entrance.

She wore her *riding jacket, her gear,* phone pressed to her ear. Focused. Composed.

We didn't speak.

And yet… the tension between us was visible, enough that even others seemed to notice.

I kept it simple. Got my change and turned to leave.

"The Walk to the Bus Stop."

A War of Memories

As I walked to the bus stop, my mind spun.

Every step felt like a rewind button pulling back the laughter, the secrets, the birthdays, the bullet rides, the late-night messages, the "I love you, machi."

I missed her. Terribly.

I considered going back. To just… apologize.

Say *"I'm sorry machi."*

Maybe it was pride, maybe fear. But something stopped me.

And then I turned to look back…

And She Was Gone

I saw her ride away on a bike not alone.

The rider wore a helmet.

I couldn't see who it was but I knew it wasn't Siddharth.

She left… with someone else. Confident. Unapologetic.

And just like that, a lump formed in my throat.

Maybe she had moved on.

Maybe the space between us was no longer a pause... but an ending.

I stood there, silently.

Watching the dust settle as the bike disappeared around the corner.

And in that moment, I realized

Sometimes, people don't wait.

Even the ones who once promised they would.

I took a deep breath.

And walked out of the college gate.

"The Notification That Spoke Louder Than Words."

As I boarded the bus and sat by the window, I took a moment to breathe. I was emotionally drained from the exam, the silence, the distance.

Then, my phone lit up with a notification. *Vijaya had posted a story.*

Curious but cautious, I opened it.

It was one of those *"best friend fight"* quotes, the kind that cuts deeper because it's vague but personal.

the kind that makes you question if the world is now being told *your story* in someone else's words.

My chest tightened.

The words stung.

Not because they were loud, but because they were silent weapons wrapped in a pretty font.

And Then I Saw Him

As I tapped through, I noticed a reaction

Siddharth had responded to her story with a *smiley hug emoji.*

Just a tiny yellow bubble.

So harmless. So subtle.

And yet… so loud.

That one emoji said everything.

He knew. She told him.

And now, I wasn't just the girl who slapped her best friend I was the outsider to their private understanding.

I felt something in my chest sink.

Not just hurt but replaced.

"The Realization."

It wasn't just about the story.

It was about how easily sides were formed, how quickly stories are shared behind screens, and how loudly silence can echo in the space where love and loyalty once lived.

Where was my side of the story?

Who would hear me without judging?

No one had asked why I reacted the way I did.

Why I felt trapped. Why I said no.

Everyone had moved forward. But I was still there in the canteen, in that moment, where everything beautiful between us fell apart with one loud silence.

"A Week of Silence."

After everything that happened, I wanted space from the drama, the noise, the expectations, and especially… social media.

Siddharth tried again.

Another friend request popped up.

This time, I didn't accept.

I didn't decline either. I just let it sit like a question I didn't want to answer.

But he didn't stop there.

He tried through his friend's account too. Still, I refused.

I wasn't angry anymore. I was exhausted.

A week of silence followed.

And for the first time in a long time, I felt *peace* a quiet that didn't ask questions, didn't force answers, didn't demand anything.

The Last Day of Exams,

It should've been a normal day.

The final exam. A breath of relief.

But then, I saw *him.*

Siddharth.

He had come to pick up Vijaya.

Helmet on. Bullet bike. The familiar posture.

But when he removed his helmet and our eyes accidentally met. I froze.

What is this?

Is this something more now?

Was I wrong about everything?

Vijaya walked up to him casually, almost comfortably.

They didn't hold hands.

There was no "moment."

But sometimes, *silence between two people says enough.*

"Confusion & Comfort"

I didn't confront. I didn't speak. I just… left.

Called the one person I knew who would listen without judging Kalyani.

"Can we meet?" I asked.

"Of course, akka," she said.

I went to her class, met her in the corridor, and the words slowly spilled out:

"I fought with Vijaya a few days back…"

I didn't tell her the whole story, just enough to hint at the weight I was carrying.

She didn't ask questions. She didn't offer opinions.

She just said,

"It's going to be okay soon."

And somehow, that was enough.

We rode home together in an auto-rickshaw not saying much, but sharing a silence that felt safe, not heavy.

"The Silence After the Storm"

Sometimes, all you need is to be heard and that night, Kalyani was exactly what I needed. No analysis. No advice. Just her presence.

Talking to my little sister gave me a sense of grounding.

It reminded me that no matter what was happening outside at college, with friends, or online, *I still had my people.*

But now, the exams are over. And so was the routine.

For the first time in weeks, there would be no reason to see Vijaya.

No canteen lunch breaks.

No morning bus stop meet-ups.

No awkward silences across exam desks. No eye contact's Nothing.

Just… space.

10 or 12 days of it. Maybe more.

I wasn't sure if I should feel relieved or anxious.

Part of me was thankful for the break.

No more emotional weight. No more unspoken tension. Maybe I could finally *breathe.*

But another part of me the quieter, softer part missed her already.

Because no matter how much went wrong, *she was still my (machi) best friend.*

"A Winter Pause"

Vacations arrived like a soft blanket wrapping me in stillness after weeks of chaos.

Though the ache of what happened with Vijaya hadn't fully faded, I began to realize something:

Sometimes, healing doesn't come from fixing what's broken.

It comes from *resting beside the brokenness*, from holding space for your own emotions.

This winter was just that.

The air was crisp, the mornings quiet.

Steam rising from a cup of coffee felt like a little ritual of comfort.

Amma's shawl smelled like home. Kalyani's giggles echoed through the hallway.

Appa's newspaper rustled just like always predictable and grounding.

In that quiet, I started to breathe differently.

Deeper. Slower.

It wasn't that everything was fine but for the first time in a while, it didn't have to be.

I gave myself permission to just *be me*.

There was no Siddharth, no Vijaya.

No social media.

No bus stop dramas. Just home.

Winter, with all its silence, became my mirror.

It reminded me that life moves in seasons:

Some friendships bloom like spring, Some hearts burn like summer,

Some truths fall like autumn leaves,

And some pains, like winter, ask us to slow down… to rest… to reflect.

And so I did.

"A Cup of Hope."

Morning, 8:45.

The scent of fresh filter coffee curled through the house like a gentle embrace. Amma stood at the stove, her hair tied back loosely, her presence radiating the kind of comfort only mothers can give. She handed me a steel tumbler filled to the brim with warmth, aroma, and quiet love.

I held it close, letting the steam kiss my face as I sat by the window.

Outside, the winter was calm. Inside, so was I.

This vacation had become a cocoon. A time to recharge. A time to rethink.

Snuggled up with books, wrapped in soft blankets, listening to old Tamil songs playing on the radio it was all soothing.

Amma would often sit beside me, sharing stories from her college days. We'd laugh, we'd listen, and sometimes, we'd just sit in silence. And yet, that silence was never empty.

As Christmas lights flickered across nearby rooftops and the whispers of a New Year approached, I began to feel a shift.

A gentle nudge in my heart.

Like life whispering,

"Maybe it's time to forgive… or at least, to try to forget."

I didn't know what would happen when college reopened.

I didn't know what I'd say to Vijaya.

But I knew one thing—*I missed her.*

And maybe that was enough to start with.

The filter coffee that morning wasn't just coffee. It was a small moment of peace, a promise of healing, and a hope that the coming year might bring back not just my best friend, but also the part of me I lost in the storm.

"An Unexpected Escape."

Around 12:30 PM.

We had just settled around the dining table, the smell of Amma's delicious sambar filling the air, when Appa dropped the bombshell. His face was beaming as he looked at us.

"We're going to your attey's Meera's place for a vacation tomorrow in Mumbai!" he announced.

I froze for a second, then a wave of excitement surged through me. *Mumbai* the city with its vibrant energy, endless lanes, and, of course, my attey's cozy house. I hadn't been there in a while, and the thought of escaping into that busy yet comforting city for a break felt like the perfect remedy.

For a moment, everything felt lighter. After all the tension, the stress of exams, and the confusion with Vijaya, I felt like this trip was a sign *a new chapter was waiting to be written.*

Kalyani and I dashed to our rooms, grabbing our bags and starting to pack furiously. Clothes, toiletries, books, Selfie stands, tripods, camera, and random things we might need. Kalyani, with her usual excitement, was already planning what we'd do in Mumbai. I could tell she was equally thrilled by the change of pace.

Kalyani's First MeTube Vlog

As we sat in the room, halfway through packing, I noticed Kalyani fumbling with her phone, a small tripod stand, and a wired mic she'd borrowed from a friend. She had a gleam in her eye, one I hadn't seen before. Focused. Eager. Almost… professional.

"What are you doing, Kallu?" I asked, folding my clothes neatly into the suitcase.

"I'm starting something new, akka!" she beamed. "My own MeTube channel! Travel vlogs, day-in-my-life, fun sister challenges we're doing all of it!"

I smiled, a little surprised but genuinely happy. "Wow, seriously? That's cool!"

She nodded enthusiastically. "Yeah! This trip to Mumbai is going to be my first vlog. I've even thought of my intro. Wanna hear it?"

I couldn't say no.

She cleared her throat, faced her phone camera, and with the sweetest nervousness, began:

practice-*"Hey everyone! This is Kalyani, and welcome to my channel!* This is my first ever video, and guess what? We're going on a family trip to Mumbai! It's going to be super fun, so come along with me!"

I watched her go through multiple takes fixing her hair, adjusting her voice, and laughing every time she messed up. It wasn't perfect, but it was real.

For the first time, I saw Kalyani not just as my little sister but as someone trying to chase a dream, in her own unique way. It felt nice to witness the beginning of something that could become big. Who knows, someday I might be proudly saying, "She started it all from our bedroom with nothing but a phone and a spark."

Vlog Mode: ON,

The next morning was a whirlwind of excitement. The bags were packed, the cab was waiting, and Appa was honking from the gate as Amma rushed around with last-minute snacks wrapped in foil.

But in the middle of all the chaos, there was Kalyani already in full *"MeTube vlogger" mode.*

She had her phone mounted on a tiny selfie stick, shades on despite the cloudy morning, and a grin that said she was ready to take the internet by storm.

"Hey everyone! What's up? This is your girl *Kalyani,* and welcome back to my channel!" she chirped into the camera. "Guess where we're going today? Yup, *Mumbai and the Lonavala baby!* Family vacation vibes. You don't wanna miss this one!"

I laughed, watching her twirl in the taxi-driveway. "Do you *have* to record every single thing?" I teased.

"Obviously," she said dramatically. "My followers love travel content. Also, your grumpy early-morning face might just go viral."

She stuck her tongue out at me, and we both burst into giggles. Amma, hearing us, shook her head. "If she spends as much time studying as she does vlogging, she'd top the board exams."

Kalyani didn't miss a beat. "That's why I'm going to be *famous*, Amma. No need for exam results when you have subscribers." Appa loudly said, you and your social media. *Uff!*

The journey began with her filming the streets zipping past the car window, shots of filter coffee at roadside stops, train travel and even snippets of our random singing in the back seat. Every moment was content for her, and somehow, it made the trip feel even more memorable.

But in between her vlogging and my silent staring out the window, I felt something slowly healing. Maybe the distraction was good. Maybe being around family, seeing Kalyani's joy, and laughing at her exaggerated commentary was exactly what I needed after the emotional turbulence of the past few weeks.

I wasn't sure if the camera captured it, but somewhere in those frames, we were all *together*, at peace, and slowly finding our way forward.

"Can't wait to see the sea! I'll take a million pictures!" she exclaimed, already thinking about her social media feed.

I couldn't help but smile. The thought of a family vacation after all the chaos was a gift in itself. Lonavala was always so peaceful and serene, a place where time seemed to slow down. And though I knew Mumbai would be bustling, Attey's Meera's place always had that soothing, homely atmosphere. Plus, we'd get a chance to go on some fun adventures together.

"A Journey of Family and Exploration."

Rediscovery in Mumbai,

The early morning train ride had me caught between two worlds leaving the comforting embrace of home and looking forward to the rush of Mumbai, with its chaotic energy and endless stories. As I sat by the window, watching the world rush by, I thought about everything I was leaving behind. But the thought of seeing my attey again made the journey feel a little lighter.

I sat on my train seat for a moment, gazing out the window at the dull gray sky of winter. There was something about this day, something quiet and comforting, that made me feel hopeful. I was ready for this change, for the new experiences, and maybe—just maybe—some clarity on the path forward.

Arriving at CST station, the moment I saw her welcoming smile, the worries of the day seemed to vanish. Attey's warmth has a way of making everything feel familiar and safe. Her farmhouse in Lonavala, Just outside Mumbai, had always felt like an escape from the busy streets of the city. With its serene surroundings, lush greenery, and the smell of fresh air, it was exactly what I needed to recharge.

During the day, we explored the stunning Marine Drive, where the skyline melted into the ocean at sunset, casting a golden hue over everything. Kalyani, on the other hand, had her own mission: snapping photos for her MeTube page, excited about capturing every detail to share with her growing audience. Even though her camera was almost always in hand, I couldn't help but notice her new sense of passion for her channel it was more than just a hobby now. I was curious to see how it would unfold.

In the evenings, we indulged in Mumbai's street food, savoring mumbai *cha zhan zhanit-vada pav* and *canon pav bhaji* with the sound of local vendors shouting their prices and tourists bargaining. But the best part was sharing the moments with my attey, who brought her own spice to everything. She could tell the history behind every monument, the legend of every street corner, and the little-known gems hidden in the city's nooks and crannies. It made Mumbai feel less overwhelming and more like a place of endless discovery.

I couldn't help but reflect on how this trip was more than just a vacation. It was a reminder that, in a world that moves faster than we often realize, there's beauty in slowing down. Family bonds are the thread that holds everything together, whether it's during busy street markets or over a quiet cup of chai.

By the time we had to leave, I wasn't just leaving Mumbai. I was leaving behind a piece of myself that had rediscovered the joy of family, tradition, and connection.

"A Night in Lonavala."

As we pulled into Lonavala around 9:45 pm, the cool air greeted us like an old friend. The noise of Mumbai faded behind us, replaced by the soft rustling of trees and the chirping of night insects. Attey Meera's farmhouse stood tall and welcoming, a two-story haven wrapped in vines and the smell of damp earth after a day's sun. The porch light glowed like a warm hug in the night.

I didn't even have the energy to unpack. I gave my attey a soft smile, exchanged a few tired words, and made my way upstairs. My room had a wooden cot with floral bedsheets, a soft breeze sneaking in through the open windows, and the comforting smell of lemongrass oil she must've lit before we arrived. I barely changed before I collapsed into bed, my body aching but my heart full.

That night, I didn't dream much. Just the gentle hum of a ceiling fan above and the fading echoes of train tracks in my ears. Sometimes, rest isn't just sleep it's surrender.

The Golden Morning in Lonavala,

The clock barely touched six when I woke to the soft clinking of stainless steel vessels and the low hum of voices Amma and Attey, lost in their world of stories. There was something soothing about that rhythm like background music to a slow, quiet morning. I stepped out to the verandah, still wrapped in my shawl, and saw the mist hovering just above the trees. The chai's aroma danced through the chilly air, inviting and familiar.

Kalyani followed a little later, camera in hand, already filming the golden light filtering through the guava trees. "Akka, look how beautiful it is!" she whispered, as though afraid to break the calm. We sat on the swing, feet tucked up, sipping chai, saying very little because sometimes, silence between siblings says more than words.

In the kitchen, the laughter from Amma and Attey grew louder. They were probably retelling old stories of marriages, mischievous cousins, and that one nosy neighbor everyone knew by name. Their gossip wasn't idle talk, it was memory-keeping, soul-healing, and deeply grounding.

I looked around and thought maybe this was the pause I needed. Away from college drama, social media noise, and confusing feelings. Here, time didn't chase me. It strolled. And for the first time in weeks, I wasn't just surviving. I was breathing.

"A Day in the Heart of Lonavala."

Attey's eyes lit up as she revealed her plan over breakfast, a surprise trip to the forest trail and the local market afterward. She was like that always blending the perfect dose of calm with excitement, turning ordinary days into sweet little adventures.

The forest trail was nothing short of magical. The towering trees stretched up like ancient guardians of the path, their branches whispering in the soft breeze. Kalyani walked ahead, camera ready, occasionally calling out, "Akka! Look, a butterfly!" or "Don't miss this angle!" I laughed every time, loving her enthusiasm.

Attey moved slowly, stopping often to show us a bright flower or mimic a bird's call. Her stories made everything come alive the old banyan tree that villagers believed was haunted, the chirpy kingfisher, and the hidden trail that led to an abandoned watchtower.

Back home, lunch was a delicious spread of hot puris, aloo sabzi, and her famous masala chaas, no southindia food- lol. We ate under the shade of the guava tree, licking our fingers and wiping tears from laughter.

Evenings were slower, gentler. The sun dipped behind the hills, painting the sky in strokes of orange and pink. We sat on the porch, with carrom boards, antakshari sessions, and gardening breaks in between. The porch buzzed with warmth, shared stories, teasing, and the soft clatter of game pieces.

Occasionally, we'd head out to scenic viewpoints. The view from the top was breathtaking the winding roads below, the mist slowly rising, the vast green expanse stretching endlessly. Standing there, I felt small… but in the best way possible. Like all my worries back home Vijaya, Siddharth, the fight, expectation suddenly shrank beneath the vastness of these hills.

And in that moment, I realized maybe it's okay to let go a little. To forgive. To not have everything figured out.

And it's a wrap,

As I stood by the gate with my bag slung over my shoulder, I looked back one last time at Attey's farmhouse its tiled roof glowing warmly in the early morning sun, the familiar scent of jasmine in the air, and Attey waving from the porch, Her smile somehow both joyful and tearful. Kalyani was already filming a goodbye snippet for her MeTube vlog, trying to hide the lump in her throat behind her cheerful narration.

The past week has healed a lot in me.

The stillness of the hills, the comfort of Amma's hand wrapped around mine during long porch talks, the unspoken kindness in Attey's gentle ways all helped calm the chaos I'd been carrying silently since that day in college.

I was no longer angry. Just… quiet. Reflective. And somehow, more open to the idea that not every fight ends everything. Some just pause it.

As the train began to pull out of Lonavala station, I texted attey, *"Next summer, same place, same porch, same chai?"* She replied with a smile emoji and a heart.

I tucked my phone away, leaned against the window, and watched the hills blur into the distance.

The train swayed gently, and I gazed out of the window, watching the scenery blur into a mix of greens and browns. I was feeling that strange blend of exhaustion and contentment, the kind that only comes from a vacation that's been both restful and meaningful. It wasn't just the places I'd visited, but the time I'd spent with Amma, Attey, and Kalyani that had left an impression on me.

I pulled my phone from my bag, scrolling through the photos I'd taken on the trip, those candid moments, the misty mornings, the cool breezes, and even the spontaneous laughter of board games at the farmhouse. I hadn't posted any updates while I was away, but now that the vacation was over, I thought it was time to share.

The app loaded, and my finger hovered over the "share" button. *Should I post these?* The quiet of the hills, the warmth of my family it all seemed so far removed from the noise of social media. I had detoxed from the constant buzz, and now I wasn't sure how to dive back into it.

I decided to share a few select pictures, ones that felt true to the spirit of the trip moments of peace and connection rather than the hustle of city life. But as I did, I couldn't shake the feeling that the digital world might never quite capture the essence of what I had experienced.

There were a few likes, some comments from friends. Vijaya had liked the photos as well, and I felt a pang in my chest. I pushed the feeling aside. It wasn't the time to think about that, not while I was heading back to a different routine, a different life. For now, I'd focus on getting home, getting back into the groove of things.

I leaned my head against the window, watching the landscape change as the train moved south. I was ready to return to Chennai, to settle back into my own space. The peace of Lonavala would stay with me, but the journey back was a reminder that life, just like travel, was all about transitions whether it's the return home, the shift in routine, or even the internal shifts I was still navigating in my relationships. Home was waiting, and with it, a chance to start fresh.

It felt strange, yet refreshing, logging back into social media after such a peaceful break. The stillness of Lonavala, the warmth of family, and the natural detox from constant updates had given me a sense of clarity. But now, as I scrolled through my feed, I saw the familiar faces and updates from my friends. There was a moment when I saw Vijaya's and

Siddharth's pictures of them riding together on a bike. It struck me with a mix of emotions, happiness for her, but also a quiet pang in my chest. She looked so free, so happy in those pictures, and I couldn't deny the feeling of missing the old connection we once shared.

But seeing her so happy, enjoying her time, made me smile too. I realized it was okay to be at peace with it. Sometimes, friendships change, and we find new connections along the way.

And then, as if on cue, I noticed that Vijaya again had liked all the pictures I posted from my trip. A simple gesture, but it felt like an unspoken acknowledgment between us. It was clear that while things had shifted, there was still a silent understanding between us. For a moment, I let myself smile, grateful that despite the distance, some connections still carried a sense of warmth.

As the evening progressed, the reality of the day of returning home, hit me. It was the 31st of December, New Year's Eve, and we had finally reached home after the long journey. The exhaustion from the travel was real, but the excitement for the new year, the fresh start it represented, kept the energy buzzing in the air.

Appa and Amma were tired, ready to unwind, but the living room was still filled with the comforting hum of laughter and conversations. We were all together, cozy, and despite the tiredness, there was a quiet sense of joy in knowing that we were starting the new year with family, with the people who matter the most.

The clock ticked closer to midnight, and the air was filled with anticipation. It wasn't the grandest New Year's Eve, but it was perfect in its simplicity. A warm home, familiar faces, and the promise of a new year ahead. I found myself reflecting on everything that had happened, the ups and downs, the quiet moments, and the personal growth.

In a way, this moment of shared calm felt like the start of something new. A fresh chapter was unfolding, and I was ready to embrace whatever came next.

"Good-Morning! - 2020"

Back to Chennai

The first morning of the new year felt different quiet, but full of potential. The soft sunlight filtered through the curtains, and the usual buzz of the world seemed a little slower, more forgiving. Amma was already up, humming to herself in the kitchen, and the familiar aroma of her morning filter coffee drifted through the house like a promise of new beginnings.

Kalyani and I sat cross-legged on the bed, scrolling through photos from the trip and shortlisting the best ones for her MeTube video. She was so animated, describing the moments behind each picture, and I loved seeing her passion come alive. It reminded me that joy often lives in small things in creativity, in memories, in shared moments with someone who just gets you.

As the new year began, I felt lighter, not because all my questions were answered or everything had fallen perfectly into place but because I had made peace with what was, and I was finally ready to look ahead. Whether or not things with Vijaya would heal, whether Siddharth would eventually move on or still linger in some corner of my story, I didn't know.

But what I did know was this - I was home. I was surrounded by love. I had dreams to chase, exams to crack, and moments yet to unfold. And for now, that was enough.

Early New Year's morning, feeling fresh with the comforting aroma of adai and tomato chutney wafting through the house, set the tone for something special. Amma's cooking always seems to carry more than just flavor it carries love, reassurance, and that gentle push to start the day right.

I was getting ready for college, with that lightness in my heart after so many emotional ups and downs, probably felt different like I was stepping into the day not just as a student, but as someone who had learned something deeper about life and relationships.

And then *that* moment near the parking area.

Vijaya saw me. and I saw her.

And without words, *we both just ran into each other's arms.*

That hug—so hard, so honest—wasn't just a gesture. It was healing. A silent understanding that everything that happened, all the hurt, all the silence, didn't change the core of what we had.

When she whispered, "Sorry," and I replied, "I'm sorry too, machi," it wasn't about who was right or wrong anymore.

It was about the *power of friendship* to *break*, *bend*, but still *mend*.

"Let's be friends again, Machi."

That line carries a quiet strength. It reminds us that *true friendship isn't about never hurting each other it's about always finding a way back.* To forgive. To forget. To move forward with love and understanding.

Such a beautiful moment to witness between us reconnecting after time apart on the occasion of New Year, mending bridges, and rediscovering the value of the bond we shared. The rawness of that emotional hug and the words, "Machi, you are my world," encapsulate everything that's been left unsaid for so long. It's the kind of moment that marks a new beginning, not just in terms of friendship but in terms of personal growth and emotional healing.

The first day of the new year brings with it a sense of renewal, like a clean slate where everything feels possible, and in this case, it was your friendship being rebuilt. The feelings you had about seeing her, your emotional response, and that simple yet profound apology they all speak volumes about how much the past weeks and months have shaped my understanding of what really matters.

I feel also absolutely right, college is not just about textbooks and exams it's about learning how to grow as a person, how to navigate the relationships that shape us, and how to embrace second chances. That's a powerful realization, and the idea of reinventing yourself each semester, regardless of what happened the year before, is an empowering one. It's as if life continuously gives us chances to start again, to learn from what's passed and to build something new from it.

As the day unfolded, it was clear that we both were stepping into this semester with a new understanding, not just of each other but also of ourselves. Our walk together through campus, reconnecting and sharing the little joys of the familiar yet new semester, felt like a promise of healing and growth.

The hum of conversations around, the laughter of classmates, the familiar faces in the classroom all of it seemed like a backdrop to the journey ahead. It was more than just a new semester; it felt like a new chapter added in my life.

The excitement, the energy of being reunited with old friends, and the anticipation of what this year could bring made me feel like we were finally back on track, both with our studies and our relationships. With each passing day, I could feel my old self coming back, the confidence I once had before the rough patches, the enthusiasm to dive into my passions, and the joy of having best friends by side once more.

As for our thoughts moving forward, it feels like this moment of reconciliation between us marked the beginning of an emotionally refreshing year. The past was behind us now, and there was so much room for us to grow together. Will there be more obstacles to overcome? Probably. Yes! But the strength I've gained from this moment, from facing fears, confronting feelings, and choosing to move forward, hoping will guide me through whatever comes next.

"Back Together, Stronger Than Before."

After that emotional reunion, Vijaya and I walked into the classroom side by side, just like in old times. The moment we stepped in, heads turned, and then... smiles. Everyone looked genuinely happy to see us together again. There was a kind of silent cheer in the air, like our friendship meant something not just to us, but to the people around us too.

We greeted everyone, and for the first time in a long while, it felt like everything was falling into place. The awkward silences, the old tensions they were gone. In their place was warmth, joy, and the comfort of being back where we belong: together, as friends. After all, we shared today the apology, the hug, the words, *"You are my world"* her silence about Siddharth felt like a shadow creeping into what was a bright, beautiful day. I didn't know what to make of it. Was she hiding something? Or was it something she didn't know how to tell me?

I didn't ask. Not yet. But the feeling lingered. {At 3 pm I came home}.

"Sharing the Good News."

After everything that unfolded with Vijaya, I couldn't keep it to myself. I had to tell someone who would understand just how much it meant. So I messaged Kalyani: *"Me and Vijaya… we're back together."* Her reply came almost instantly, full of happiness and warmth. I could almost picture her smiling as she read it. *"I'm so happy for you both!"* she said. And in that moment, it felt even more real. Telling her made it feel official like a chapter truly reopening.

"A Strange Pause in a Perfect Day"

Few week's later, Just when everything felt right again, something unexpected happened. Vijaya got a call from Siddharth. The moment she saw his name, her expression changed. She stepped aside to answer, speaking in hushed tones. And what struck me most was... she didn't say a word about it afterward.

"Letting Go, with a Smile."

A few days later in the canteen, Vijaya showed me a picture. There was a softness in her eyes, and a little nervous smile on her face. *"His name is Arun,"* she said. *"He came back into my life… and I'm seeing him again."*

For a moment, I didn't know what to feel. A part of me paused maybe from surprise, maybe from old memories but then I looked at her, truly looked, and saw how happy she was.

And that's all that mattered.

I smiled back and said, *"I'm really happy for you Machi."* And I meant it. Because sometimes, love isn't about holding on. It's about being glad when the people you care about find peace, even if it's not with you. Vijaya deserved happiness, and if Arun brought that into her life, then I was grateful for him too.

"A Story of Second Chances, Courage, and Unspoken Bonds"

Even after reuniting with me, Vijaya couldn't help but care for Siddharth, maybe not out of love, but out of a sense of unfinished story. Knowing I traveled alone every day by local bus, Vijaya asked Siddharth to take the same route. "Get to know her," she said. But Siddharth always hesitant, always afraid and missed out for two whole months. I was again upset with vijaya, I could see she was desperately helping siddharth. But I didnt react this time, somehow I was again upset with her move. That's an honest and very human reaction. It's hard when someone close to you especially someone like Vijaya, who has such a strong emotional history and starts making decisions on your behalf, even with good intentions. Feeling upset is completely valid, especially when it touches something as personal as your boundaries and emotions.

"A Line Crossed"

Just when things felt like they were settling, I sensed something again something off. Vijaya was trying to help Siddharth talk to me. I don't know if she meant well, or if she thought she was doing the right thing, but it didn't sit right with me. I trusted her. We had rebuilt something fragile and real. But this? It felt like a quiet betrayal. Like she was pulling strings behind the scenes without asking how I felt about it.

I wasn't angry just because of Siddharth. I was hurt because Vijaya didn't talk to *me* first. Didn't ask if I was ready, or if I even wanted that kind of help.

It made me question: was she really hearing me, or just doing what *she* thought was best?

"Fading Into the Background"

Every day, Siddharth started showing up by Vijaya's side, at the rides, at the bus stop. Slowly, it wasn't just her anymore. It was *them*. And something about that made me feel like I was watching my place in her life slip away.

I wanted to be okay with it. I tried. But I couldn't shake the feeling that I no longer belonged in their world. So I did what I've always done when things get too heavy, I pulled away. I started ignoring them, one moment at a time.

Not out of anger. Out of self-preservation.

It's strange how quickly someone can go from being your person to just another face in the crowd. And sometimes, it's not about what they did it's about what you feel they stopped doing. Until one day, Vijaya had enough. She gave him a push *literally* and said, *"Go talk to her. Or one day, she'll get married to someone, and it'll be too late for everything."* That day, Siddharth boarded the bus. And Vijaya left with Arun on the bike.

"The Empty Seat"

That day, I was already sitting on the window seat, the one I always loved. The breeze, the passing streets, the way it lets you drift into your own world. But this time, it felt different. The seat beside me stayed empty. Vijaya and Siddharth were at the stop too. They saw me. I saw them. But no one said anything. It's strange how silence can say everything.

"The Moment Before"

The bus hadn't started yet. The engine was silent, just like the space between me and the world around me. I sat by the window, watching the crowd settle, the usual chaos slowly calming into routine.

No one sat beside me.

Vijaya and Siddharth were nearby, chatting softly down at the bus stop. I could hear their voices, not the words, just the sound. It wasn't meant for me anymore. The driver was still outside, probably finishing his tea or waiting for the last few passengers. But inside the bus, time stretched. That moment before the journey begins felt like it would never end. And maybe, a part of me didn't want it to.

Because once the bus starts, everything moves forward. And I wasn't sure if I was ready to move on just yet.

I watched people come and go. I watched them take seats next to strangers. And yet, mine remained untouched. A part of me wished someone would sit there. A bigger part of me was glad they didn't because I wasn't sure if I was ready to let anyone that close again.

That empty seat? It wasn't just beside me. It was inside me too.

He didn't sit next to me, though he wanted to I felt. He could but he couldn't. Because on that same ride, someone was harassing a girl from my college. Something inside Siddharth snapped. He stood up, and he fought. He didn't care about the pain, the blood, or who was watching. He chose to protect a stranger over chasing his own moment. That fight sent him to the hospital.

"A Glimpse That Said Everything"

Just as the bus workers were helping Siddharth out his body still weak from the earlier fight, I caught a glimpse of something that froze me.

His phone slipped slightly from his hand, and for a second, just a fleeting second, I saw it. My Social media display picture was his phone's wallpaper.

Everything around me blurred the chatter, the footsteps, even the sound of the engine finally starting. All I could focus on was that screen. That single image said everything he hadn't dared to. Even after all the silence. Even after all the distance.

He never changed it.

And in that quiet second, sitting by the window, something inside me cracked because I didn't know whether to feel seen, guilty, or just... lost

I was shocked, when I saw my own photo as his screensaver while he lay injured, something shifted in my heart. Maybe it was admiration. Maybe it was love. But from that day on, I saw him differently. I loved his action, And I realized Vijaya told me that he is a good human being.

Siddharth began showing up at the bus stop every day after that day, waiting, hoping, yet still too scared to speak. I was so scared and Vijaya left me all alone. She finally found one friend, and got busy with him.

"When He Finally Spoke"

One day, out of nowhere, he walked up to me.

His voice was low, hesitant. "Hey…"

It wasn't much, but it carried the weight of everything left unsaid of bus rides, empty seats, silent glances, and my photo still clinging to his lock screen.

I looked at him. I didn't feel anger anymore. Just a quiet understanding.

I smiled soft, honest and said, *"You really did a very good job that day."*

He blinked, a little surprised, like he hadn't expected kindness. But he smiled back. And in that simple moment, no explanations were needed. The walls we built slowly began to come down not with apologies, but with acknowledgment and grace.

"Choosing Silence."

After our short exchange, Siddharth looked lighter almost like he'd been holding his breath for months and could finally let go. He smiled, then left the college. There was a calm in his steps, and somehow, it made me feel calm too.

But the peace didn't last long.

Later that day at 8:30, I saw Vijaya arguing with Arun near the college entrance. Her voice wasn't loud, but her face said enough hurt, frustration, something breaking beneath the surface. I froze for a moment, watching from afar.

My instinct told me to text her: *Is everything okay?* My heart told me to step in.

But I didn't.

I held back.

Not because I didn't care but because I was learning. Learning that sometimes people need space to fight their own battles, and that caring doesn't always mean intervening.

So I just watched. Quietly. And walked away, carrying the weight of a message never sent.

"Words I Didn't Say."

That day, I really wanted to tell her about Siddharth. That we finally spoke. That I smiled. Maybe, finally something between us had softened. It felt important. Like a step forward worth sharing.

But when I saw her face tense, eyes stormy, arguing with Arun, I knew it wasn't the right time. She looked like she was carrying too much already. My words, no matter how well-intentioned, would've been just another weight.

So I held them in.

I walked past with a nod, not a sentence. Sometimes the hardest thing is not what you say, but what you choose *not* to say.

And in that silence, I hoped she'd understand that I was still there just giving her space to breathe.

"WORRY DOESN'T WAIT."

Though I'd been upset with Vijaya for a while, the anger had faded. We were still best friends (Machi's) even if the distance between us was unspoken. But when I saw her story that day, something shifted. It looked sad. Off. Like something was quietly breaking inside her.

And suddenly, none of the past mattered. The fights, the silence, the things we didn't say they all disappeared in that one moment of worry.

I picked up my phone. I didn't overthink it. I just called her. Because no matter what happened before…when someone you love looks like they're drowning, you don't wait to be invited. You jump in.

"A Heart on the Line."

When she picked up, her voice was heavy, slurred, fragile. I could tell right away: she'd been drinking. And when she finally started talking, it all came pouring out.

"It was about *likes*, you know?" she said, almost laughing at how silly it sounded. "Arun keeps liking some other girl's pictures on social media… and when I asked him about it, he said he doesn't care whatever you say."

Her voice cracked. That last part *he doesn't care* hit her the hardest.

It was about jealousy. It wasn't even about the pictures. It was about what those pictures represented. Neglect. Disrespect. Being made to feel replaceable in a space where she wanted to feel secure. "I thought he cared," she whispered, as if even she wasn't sure anymore.

And as I sat there, phone pressed to my ear, listening to the same girl who once told me *I was her world*, I realized sometimes the strongest people fall the hardest. And all we can do is be there to catch them.

"A Silent Promise."

S he hung up the phone, and for a second, there was only silence. But then, her last words echoed in my mind: *"I'll call you back soon. I'll bounce back soon."*

It was hard to know if she believed it or if she was just trying to convince herself. But in that fragile moment, I knew one thing she wasn't ready to give up. Not on herself. Not on what she had with Arun. She was hurt, but that wouldn't define her.

I waited, knowing that sometimes the best thing you can do for someone is to give them space to heal. And when she was ready, she'd reach out.

"I'll bounce back soon." Those words stayed with me, like a quiet promise hanging in the air, as I settled into my own thoughts, hoping that whatever path she took, she'd find her strength again.

Two day's later,

She was absent for lectures, I tried to reach her out, but her phone was out of service. I was worried for her, so I waited. I didn't had an option. When she finally called back, there was a soft, almost hesitant tone in her voice, like she wasn't sure what to say. But this time, I didn't hold back. I needed her to know, needed to share this piece of truth.

"I talked to Siddharth," I said. *"I smiled. We spoke while getting off the bus."*

There was a quiet pause on the other end. I could almost hear her processing it, maybe surprised by the simple honesty of it. But then, slowly, she spoke. *"I'm glad... really,"* she said, and I could hear the relief in her voice. It was a relief for both of us, in a way like that small, quiet step was finally breaking the tension we'd both been carrying.

"Clear Words, Open Hearts."

She was happy when I told her about Siddharth that we spoke, that I let go of the weight between us, at least a little. But I knew I had to say more. Something I had been carrying quietly inside.

"Machi," I said gently, *"I still want to stay away…not completely, but just enough. I can be a good friend to him. But not a girlfriend. Not now, maybe not ever."*

There was a pause. A soft, thoughtful silence on the other end of the call.

Then she replied, *"I'm happy you chose to be his friend at least. That means something. That's enough."*

And in that moment, I felt it *peace.* No pressure, no confusion. Just two people who cared deeply, finally understanding each other's truth.

"The Weekend That Drifted."

January 26, 2020, rolled around Republic Day. A long weekend lay ahead, with Friday, Saturday, and Sunday all lined up like a much-needed break from the chaos. Vijaya mentioned she was heading out for a ride something spontaneous, something she needed. I wished her well, even if I felt a little distant.

That morning, my phone's display completely gave up. Just a black screen where connection used to live. I couldn't see calls, messages, or stories. I couldn't reach out.

So I walked down to the repair shop and handed it over. "It'll take a day or two," they said. Those two days felt longer than they should have. In the middle of a holiday meant for freedom and ease, I suddenly felt completely out of the loop with everyone, and especially with her.

And somewhere deep down, I wondered: *what if something important happens while I'm unreachable?* But all I could do was wait.

"A Disconnected Monday."

Monday morning came, and I was supposed to collect my phone. It had been three days of silence, no calls, no messages, no updates. I left early, empty pockets where my phone used to be, and a strange stillness in my chest.

College felt different without it. Quieter. Slower.

And then I noticed, Vijaya wasn't there. Her seat was empty. No smile. No wave. Just space.

Usually, I wouldn't overthink it. Maybe she was tired. Maybe the ride wore her out. But today… with no way to check in, no messages to scroll back to, her absence felt loud.

I looked around, hoping to spot her somewhere. Nothing.

And all I could do was wait until the repair shop opened, wait for the screen to light up again, to see if any message, any missed call, any clue was waiting for me.

"Silence Speaks Too."

By afternoon, I finally had my phone back in my hand. For a moment, I felt a small surge of hope. Maybe there would be a missed call, a message, something from Vijaya. Some signs on social media. But there was nothing. No notifications. No texts. No calls. Just a quiet screen, like the world had moved on without me.

I dialed her number. It rang. And rang. But she didn't pick up.

I typed out a short message—*"Hey, I saw you weren't in college today. Everything okay?"* and hit send.

Then I waited. And waited. Hours passed. Still no reply.

The worst part wasn't the silence. It was *not knowing* what that silence meant. Was she okay? Was she angry? Or just… gone somewhere, emotionally, without updating me?

By evening, the unanswered message stared back at me like a closed door. And all I could do was sit with the questions.

Then suddenly, Vijaya disappeared, her phone were off, no social media updates, no nothing. No one saw her at exams. No posts, no messages. Just silence. I was worried, tried to find her until a college security guard came to me in the evening and said, *"Vijaya met with an accident. She's in the hospital. Needs O-Negative blood—rare. And how come a best friend doesn't know?"*

I ran breathless, desperate to the hospital. I saw Siddharth again, caring for Vijaya, surrounded by her friends and family. Without hesitation, I stepped forward and donated her blood saving the life of the girl she once distanced herself from. Every day after that, I visited her after college. Sat by Vijaya's bed. Held her hand. Said the words that had been building up: *"I'm sorry. I should've been there. But, I never stopped caring."*

And Vijaya, through her weakness and tears, said, *"I made mistakes too.*

But I'm glad you're here now."

The friendship once cracked was now stronger than ever. We found healing in forgiveness, and strength in each other. And somewhere in the background, Siddharth still stood quietly, carrying the weight of a heart that chose others before himself.

"Love in a Time of Goodbyes."

Vijaya tried again to convince me to speak with my parents, to listen to heart before it's too late. But this time, there was a shift. A truth unveiled.

"I'm getting married soon," I said softly. *"It's what my parents want. After the exams, it'll all be over." And I left the hospital.*

Vijaya then immediately told Siddharth, as he was sitting with arun outside the room. *"Bro, You don't have much time. If you really love her… you need to act. Now." He looked confused. He said, enna??*

(what happen).

"The Truth Unfolds"

A Conversation That Ended Something. The hospital was quieter than usual just the soft hum of machines and muffled voices in the background. Siddharth sat beside Vijaya, the two of them wrapped in an odd calm, somewhere between exhaustion and acceptance.

She looked at him, eyes heavy, but steady.

"I haven't told many people yet," she began. *"But… Vellankanni is getting married soon. After exams. It's all arranged."*

He didn't say anything right away. His face didn't change. But something behind his eyes flickered like another light quietly turning off.

"So it's happening," he said, almost to himself.

Vijaya nodded. *"I'm not sure how you feel, but I understand everything"* she added sincerly. *"But, I honestly wanted you both to be together.*

Siddharth Sadly looked down at the floor for a long moment. Then up at her.

"She deserve someone who sees her fully," he said softly. *"But if She've chosen peace over love, I get it. I really do."* There was silence between them deep, still, and full of everything they wouldn't say. And in that moment, they both knew:

some stories don't end in drama or chaos. Some just end in acceptance.

He was silent, confused. The weight of it lingered in the air unspoken words, glances that meant more, and silence that said everything.

"The Healing Days"

Every day after college, Siddharth and I made our way to the hospital.

It became a part of our routine, almost sacred. No matter how long the lectures ran, or how tired we felt, we always ended the day the same way: by her side.

Vijaya was recovering, and it showed. The pale look on her face was gone, replaced by her usual spark. She laughed more now, complained about the hospital food, teased the nurses, and even scolded Siddharth for bringing her junk snacks. But more than that, she *felt* like herself again. And in those small moments, those ordinary, beautiful moments I remembered why we loved her so much. Arun and Siddharth also became very good buddies.

Sometimes, all three of us would just sit in silence, sharing space more than words. There was no pressure to explain anything anymore. The past was still there, but it didn't weigh us down like before.

We were healing, in different ways.

She from her wounds.

Siddharth from his heartbreak.

And me from the distance we once let grow between us.

And though none of us said it aloud, we knew this quiet companionship was saving us all.

"Falling, Slowly"

Somewhere in the middle of those hospital visits... something started changing. It wasn't planned. It wasn't dramatic. It was quiet, almost unnoticeable. I started falling for Siddharth. Not because he said the right things or tried to be charming. But because he didn't have to. He was just *there*. Every single day. He looked after Vijaya like family, not with any hidden motive, but out of pure care.

While Arun drifted in and out, distracted, detached, Siddharth was constant. He remembered her favorite snacks. Adjusted her pillows without asking. Sat through boring hours just to make sure she felt less alone.

And through it all, he never made it about himself.

It was those little things. The way he spoke with the hospital staff. The way he checked if I had eaten when he knew I hadn't. The way he'd laugh with me just enough, but never too much.

His gentleness wasn't weakness, it was strength. The quiet kind. The kind that makes you feel safe without ever saying a word.

And before I realized it fully, I wasn't just watching him anymore, I was *feeling* something.

Maybe it wasn't love just yet.

But it was more than friendship.

Siddharth and I were slowly building something fragile, something tender. It started in the hospital itself with quiet conversations, shared tea, long silences that felt full instead of empty. And I finally accepted his friend request on social media. That was the first yes.

Soon, the two of us were inseparable after college hospitals turned into hangouts, and then came the question: *"Can I take you out… just for a day?"*

I said no.

Then changed it to yes, with limits.

He took me to Marina Beach in Chennai. The sea breeze, the chaos of the city, and his hopelessly charming ways he was all heart.

"When Silence Turned to Storm"

Siddharth had gone down to the canteen to buy juice for me. He smiled before leaving, said, *"I'll be right back, don't move."*

I nodded, absentmindedly scrolling through my phone.

Then, it happened. A man, someone unfamiliar, maybe a visitor approached. At first, I thought he was just passing by. But then, his eyes lingered too long. His smile was too forced. And in the next moment, he said something crude under his breath words I can't repeat. He moved a little too close. I froze. My voice caught in my throat. There were people around, but no one noticed. Or maybe they didn't care.

And then,

Before I could even react, Siddharth was there. He had seen it from across the shop. Juice cup still in hand, eyes blazing. He didn't even speak. Just pulled me gently behind him and faced the man.

"Say one more word," Siddharth said, voice low and firm. *"And I'll make sure you leave this hospital on a stretcher."* The man mumbled something and backed off, disappearing before anyone could blink.

I looked at Siddharth. Not just at what he did, but *how* he did it. Calm. Protective. Furious, but still in control.

He handed me the juice, hands shaking slightly.

"Are you okay?" he asked softly.

I nodded, still holding my breath. *But inside, my heart wasn't calm anymore.*

That was the moment I knew.

This wasn't just admiration.

I was falling—*hard.*

A man tried to misbehave with me at the beach, and Siddharth didn't hesitate. He fought. Protected me. That day at that moment, I knew that I am in love. I texted this to Machi, Vijju. I think I am in love.

Later that night, he offered to drop me home on his bike. I agreed. But my Appa saw us from the bedroom's window, we were standing close, laughing softly. The window became a wall.

"One Call, a Thousand Fears"

Just as the air was beginning to settle, and my hands stopped trembling from what had just happened, I heard it.

"Vellankanni!" "Vellankanni!" Appa's voice. Loud. Sharp. Unmistakable. It echoed from across the house's corridor like thunder crashing through calm skies. *"Come home. Now."*

My heart dropped.

I turned and saw him standing at the end of the hallway, arms crossed, face unreadable but burning with fury. In that one moment, everything around me blurred. Siddharth's protective presence. The juice still clutched in my hand. The racing of my heart not just from fear, but from all the emotions that had quietly been building up.

I took a deep breath, glanced once at Siddharth. He looked stunned, but he didn't say a word. He just gave me that same look he always did steady, supportive, like no matter what happened next, he was on my side.

But I knew what that voice meant.

It meant questions.

It meant control.

It meant another wall between me and the one person who made me feel seen.

And I walked toward it anyway. I had no option. Because that's what daughters sometimes do walk back into silence, even when their heart is screaming to stay.

"Silence, Loud Enough"

Appa didn't say a word when I reached home. No questions. No accusations. Not a single sentence. But he didn't need to. The way he had screamed my name it said everything.

It said, *"I saw you."*

It said, *"I know."*

It said, *"This should end now."*

And the silence that followed was louder than any shouting match. He didn't look at me during dinner. Didn't ask about college. Didn't ask if I was okay. But his silence was deliberate. Heavy. A quiet punishment.

I sat there, feeling the walls close in again. Everything that had felt free my laughter, my feelings for Siddharth, that fragile sense of choice was suddenly under lock and key. And all I could do was pretend to be okay. Because when Appa doesn't speak, it's not calm. It's out of control. And I felt every word he didn't say.

"A Ride I Didn't Ask For"

The next morning around 7:30, as I stepped into the kitchen, the silence from last night still hung heavy in the air. Appa was sitting at the table, reading the paper like nothing had happened. Then, without looking up, he said, *"I'll drop you to college today."* His tone was firm. Not a suggestion or an instruction. I paused for a moment, heart thudding. I wanted to ask *why now?* But I already knew the answer.

(It wasn't care.

It wasn't convenient.

It was a message.)

I see you. I'm watching. Stay in line.

I swallowed hard and nodded.

"Ok, Appa."

That was all I said.

The car ride was quiet. No music. No conversation. Just the sound of tires on the road and thoughts spinning too loud inside my head. I looked out the window, trying not to think of Siddharth. Trying not to feel everything I wasn't allowed to feel. When we reached college, Appa didn't say bye. Just a nod. A look. And then he drove away. But that look stayed with me all day. As I walked through the college gate, the weight of the morning still on my shoulders, my phone buzzed.

Once.

Then again. And again.

Vijaya.

Back-to-back calls. My screen lit up with her name like it was trying to shake me out of everything I was holding in. She must've finally seen the message I sent her last night. The one I wrote in the dark, feeling scared and small after Appa's voice thundered through the house. I hadn't said much. Just a few words *"Appa saw us, I don't know what's happening anymore. I'm scared of my father now."*

Now she was calling. Over and over. Like she already understood more than I could put into words. I didn't answer right away. I just stared at the screen, feeling a lump rise in my throat. Because sometimes when someone cares that much, you don't know how to let them in. But I knew one thing. I needed to hear her voice. And maybe just maybe tell her everything.

Before I could gather the words, before I could press call or type another message, She texted me saying, I know everything machi, Please answer my call. Siddharth had already told her everything. He must've seen the fear in my eyes when Appa called my name. The way I left without a word. He told her I wasn't okay. So when I saw her name flash on my screen again, I knew. She wasn't calling to ask what happened. She already knew. She was calling because she couldn't sit still knowing I was sad. And that's when I realized Siddharth didn't break my trust. He protected me in a way I didn't even know I needed.

Vijaya's messages flooded in.

"Call me."

"I heard what happened."

"I'm here, okay? Just call me."

For the first time in days, I felt something crack open.

This wasn't just friendship. This was family the kind of family we choose.

And I finally picked up the phone. Saying, *"Machi, I love him. But, this can't happen. I'm getting married. Appa won't accept us ,he's not Brahmin. He'll never allow it."*

"The Voice That Calmed the Storm"

When I finally answered the call, I couldn't speak right away. But I didn't have to. Vijaya's voice came through, soft and steady like she already knew what I needed. She said, *"It's okay, machi. Just breathe. I'm here."*

I closed my eyes, sitting on the edge of the college steps, letting the tension start to loosen, just a little. *"I know Appa saw you. Siddharth told me everything. But listen, no pressure. No guilt. No explanations. Let's just... stay out of this for now."* I didn't fully understand what "this" meant, maybe the drama, maybe the pain, maybe the expectations. But in that moment, I didn't need to.

She was telling me:

You don't have to carry all of it. Not alone. Let's be friends.

And I believed her.

I nodded, wiping the quiet tear from my cheek.

"Okay, Vijaya. Let's stay out of this." And for the first time in days, I felt like I could exhale.

"Split in Two."

As we spoke on the phone, her voice calm but distant, I noticed it. A pause. A slight break in her words. Then the sound of her screen lighting up. She asked me to wait, as she was getting a second call from Siddharth.

"Another call".

She went quiet for a second, then said, half-distracted, *"Siddharth's calling again."* There it was. The sting she tried to hide. *"You can take it,"* I offered, gently.

"Yes Machi, it's okay. Let it ring. He probably just wants to check on you anyway."

And in that one line, She heard it all.

"A Line Drawn in Pain."

Siddharth's name flashed on her screen again. She didn't hesitate this time she picked up.

"Hello?" Enna? Eppadi irrukai Sid?

His voice was hurried, hopeful.

"Vijaya, is Vellankanni okay? She didn't answer my texts. Is she in college today? I need to talk to her please."

There was a pause.

A deep breath from her side. I am home, as the doctor asked me to rest for a week.

Then her voice, steady but sad.

"Bro… you're late."

He didn't respond right away. So she continued.

"Her Appa's already made up his mind. The marriage talks have started. Her father has recently visited the guy's house in lonavala. And she's not fighting back anymore. She's tired, and scared."

Siddharth's silence screamed louder than any words could.

"Look," she said gently, *"I know how much you care and love her. I do. But you need to understand… She's not just dealing*

with love. She's dealing with a wall built by generations. And right now? I don't want to lose both of you."

He sighed.

"So you're saying I should stop?"

"I'm saying," Vijaya said softly, *"if you really love her, you'll respect what she can't say out loud."*

And that was it.

A door closed not because love ran out, but because the world around it left no room.

"Loving from Afar"

Vijaya expressed, Siddharth wasn't the kind of boy to quit.

Not when it came to love.

Not when it came to *her*. (vellankanni)

He had fallen for Vellankanni with the kind of heart that didn't know how to unlove. He wanted to fight for her. To stand at her door with flowers and fury. To face her father and say, *"I'll take care of her better than anyone ever could."*

But he didn't.

Because sometimes, loving someone means knowing when your presence becomes a burden.

And so… he stayed away.

He stopped calling.

Stopped asking questions.

Stopped showing up at the bus stop where they used to steal glances like secrets.

But his silence wasn't cold, it was *loud* with love.

He still thought about her when he passed Marina Beach. Still waited an extra minute outside college hoping to catch a glimpse. Still wrote unsent messages late at night.

He wasn't waiting for a miracle.

He was simply keeping space in his heart that no one else could fill.

Because boys, when they really fall in love, then they don't just leave. They *stay*, even when they're gone. That's a dramatic twist,

"The Story That Had Just Begun... Ended."

Siddharth just found out from vijaya that I also love him, and now he's hit with the news that my father has arranged my marriage with someone else in Lonavala, at my attey's place. This sets up a lot of emotional tension and urgency.

Depending on Siddharth's personality, he was heartbroken, anger, desperate, or even resolved to fight for the relationship. And for me, this was a moment of inner conflict between family duty and true love.

Siddharth couldn't breathe. He ran to his mother. Begged her to visit my appa. They both came to my house unexpectedly. The air was thick with tension as Siddharth stepped into the house with his mother by his side. He had rehearsed his words a hundred times, but nothing could prepare him for the sharp chill in Appa's stare.

Appa sat firmly in the center of the room, spine straight, arms crossed. His face was unreadable. Siddharth spoke first, voice respectful but clear. "Uncle, I've come today with my mother... not to challenge your wishes, but to ask *humbly* to consider me. I love Vellankanni."

His mother added softly, "Our families may come from different traditions, sir, but we come with respect and sincere intentions."

A heavy silence followed.

Appa stood, his voice cutting through the air like a blade. "You are not Brahmin. You do not belong to our caste. I am not looking for love marriages. I have already spoken to my sister in Lonavala. The wedding is being arranged."

Siddharth's heart dropped. His eyes flicked toward me, who stood in the hallway, silent tears in my eyes.

Appa's voice rose, colder now. "Please leave my house."

Siddharth clenched his jaw, nodded slightly not out of agreement, but restraint. With a last glance at me, he turned and walked out, his mother quietly following. They came but they returned insulted, humiliated. No mercy. No acceptance.

Outside, the sky was beginning to darken, as if mourning with them.

The story that had just begun… ended.

We both were broken. Both of them confided in Vijaya over a video call who quietly took it all in.

Vijaya sat on the edge of her bed, still in her half-packed saree for her cousin's wedding in "Thiruvottiyur". But her mind wasn't on celebrations. She had seen the look in my eyes, that mix of love, helplessness, and silent protest. It haunted her.

{She texted Vellankanni}.

"Meet Me on the Terrace. Urgent."

Fifty five minutes later, I went, wrapped in a shawl, my face looked pale from crying. Vijaya pulled me in and said, "Enough is enough. I've seen how much you love him. And I've seen how much this is breaking you."

My voice trembled. "But Appa... he won't listen. He's already planned everything."

Vijaya smirked slightly, her eyes lighting up with a mix of mischief and defiance. "Well then... let's *unplan* it. You think I'm just going to this wedding to smile and throw flowers? No. I'm going there to make room

for *you two*. I'll stall, I'll distract, I'll gather info whatever it takes."

I looked at Vijaya, stunned. "Are you serious?"

Vijaya grinned. "Dead serious. You get Siddharth ready. This isn't over. Not by a long shot."

A few weeks later, she planned a trip to "Thiruvottiyur." for her cousin's wedding. She convinced my parents it was family, cousins wedding, nothing more. Somehow appa amma always trusted her, they allowed me to go with machi, as she was more than a family friend now. (But, Appa was unaware that Siddharth join the Thiruvottiyur wedding trip)

Siddharth, Myself, Vijaya, and Arun (Vijaya's boyfriend from a dating app) all went together. The trip was filled with laughter, sunsets, shared rooms, stolen glances. Siddharth was glowing, charming, poetic, full of love. Every gesture, every smile, every laugh was just for me. I loved everything he use to do to make me smile. He always treated me like a princess. Like I was everything.

And somewhere, as Vijaya watched us from the side, her smile faded just a little. She laughed with us during the wedding. She posed for photos. But inside, something was stirring.

She missed love.

She missed being seen the way Siddharth looked at me. (I suppose)

She missed having someone to call her *world.*

And even as Arun held her hand… she felt a distance that couldn't be crossed.

One evening, when the noise finally faded and it was just the two of them—Vijaya and Siddharth—She sat down across from him. He looked tired, emotionally drained. The way someone looks when they've been holding onto hope for too long. He was happy because I was around him. And then

Vijaya spoke. "*Siddharth, I need to tell you everything,*" she said quietly. Siddharth looked up, *worried.*

She took a deep breath. "*Vellankanni love's you.*" Maybe it still does. But her world was too heavy too full of rules, traditions, and expectations. Her father saw you both together that night… and from that moment, everything shifted. She didn't want to leave you. She is scared she'd lose her family if she chose you."

She paused. Her voice cracked.

"She texted you because it was the only way she could end it without falling apart. And you… you didn't deserve that silence. I'm sorry I didn't tell you sooner."

Siddharth sat still. The pain in his eyes softened into something else understanding, maybe. Or the final kind of heartbreak, the one that comes with closure. Vijaya looked at him for a long moment, and then added, almost as a whisper:

"And you know what hurts the most? Watching you love her the way I wish someone would love me." *And she laughed.*

In that single confession, the past, present, and everything unsaid finally came to the surface.

"When Love Turns to Shadows."

Vijaya had always been our biggest supporter.

She was the bridge between me and Siddharth when we couldn't speak. She was the one who said, *"If you love each other, don't let anything stop you."* She was the heart that held us together.

But sometimes, the strongest hearts crack the deepest.

Her own love stories kept falling apart one after another. Arun had drifted away. The boys before him had left her feeling disposable, like love was a thing people just took and left behind.

And when she saw the quiet closeness forming between me and Siddharth… it stung.

Not because she didn't want us to be happy.

But because she was tired of being *the one watching happiness happen to someone else.*

She missed the kind of love that left sweet messages, brought snacks without asking, and fought silently for your safety.

She missed being seen. The jealousy. The ache. The exhaustion of being the one always holding things together for others, while quietly falling apart herself. She didn't hate us. She hated that somewhere along the way, she felt left out of love. And as her silence stretched, I knew this wasn't about Siddharth anymore. This was about *her*.

About everything she was losing inside herself.

And in that mess of emotions jealousy, sadness, rage something snapped.

Out of anger, she did something unthinkable.

"Late Night After the Wedding."

The music had died down. The fairy lights blinked dully against the midnight mist. Guests were either asleep or slumped over half-finished drinks.

Arun slept off, But Vijaya wasn't asleep. She sat alone on the balcony of the guesthouse, an empty wine glass dangling from her fingers. Her emotions were on fire: regret, rage, helplessness.

She opened her phone, her fingers trembling. Her eyes were bloodshot, her thoughts chaotic.

"I tried to help them... and this is what happened?" she mumbled. "*They* deserves better. *She* deserves better."

She opened a new Social media account. Username: *real_vellankanni_fun.*

Display name: *Vellankanni Fun.*

Profile pic: A stolen selfie from my chatapp DP. Bio: *Available for you.*

Then, she started posting:

Old photos of me.

Quotes about sex against society.

A story: "What if your parents loved their caste more than your happiness?"

The account started gaining attention quickly. Relatives, friends, even some wedding guests saw it. Rumors spread.

By morning, the digital damage was done and I had no idea what storm was waiting.

She created a fake version of me.

A profile.

A rumor.

A shadow. So much in one night.

It didn't make sense. It wasn't who she was. But pain doesn't always act in reason. And in trying to hurt the love she envied, she ended up hurting herself more.

"Railway Station – Early Morning."

The sky was still gray with dawn as me and Siddharth boarded the train at Thiruvottiyur. There was no loud farewell, no tears at the platform, just silence, stillness, good memories. Just me and siddharth, and a quiet hope that maybe this new beginning might come without a storm.

Siddharth looked at me as the train pulled away. "Are you sure about this?"

I nodded slowly, my hand finding his. "We're not running away from them. We're running *toward* what we deserve." *He smiled.*

Back at the (wedding) guesthouse, Vijaya was fast asleep, her phone buzzing repeatedly beside her pillow comments, DMs, and tags lighting up the fake account she had made. She herself was unaware of what she did last night. Meanwhile, Screenshots had already been forwarded to my Appa, to relatives, and even to some of Siddharth's extended family.

What had started as an impulsive act of anger was now spreading fast and neither myself nor Siddharth had any clue about this act. We both were busy enjoying our trip back to Anna nagar.

"Somewhere between Thiruvottiyur and Anna Nagar – on the Train."

The rhythmic clatter of the train wheels felt strangely comforting. I sat beside Siddharth, my head resting on his shoulder, My fingers laced with his. For the first time in weeks, maybe months, there was peace. No rules, no caste talks, no disapproving glances, just two people reclaiming a piece of their own story.

Siddharth gently brushed a strand of hair from my face. *He said, "you look tired. Get some sleep. I'll wake you if anything comes up."*

I smiled. "Not sleepy. Just... peaceful."

He handed me a bottle of water and adjusted the small pillow behind my back. "You've been through too much. We'll figure out everything else later. One step at a time." *I smiled, and told him Sid this is not possible in this life. He then asked me to close my eyes and sleep for a while.*

Our phones had no signal, nothing but a dead network icon in the top corner of the screen. Messages aren't delivered. Notifications were paused. The world felt paused.

But in that pause, something unexpected was brewing.

"The Words That Got Stuck."

I was always good at hiding my emotions. Good at staying strong for everyone around me especially for my family, for Vijaya, and for Siddharth. But when it came to confessing the one thing that truly mattered *my feelings for Siddharth I* couldn't find the words. And I choose to be silent, because nothing was possible.

It wasn't that I didn't feel it.

I felt it with every glance I shared, every late-night conversation in this trip, every quiet moment we had spent together. But now, with the weight of my father's expectations, my heart had become a cage. I had waited too long. And now, with the marriage talks looming over me like a storm, the moment to tell him felt like it had passed.

But I never told him that I love him and respect him even more, what I really felt.

"I love you, Siddharth. I always will."

Those words were stuck in my throat, tangled with fear and doubt. I wanted to say him, and wanted to let him know that I wasn't as sure about this arranged marriage as my parents thought. But I didn't know if I would be able to marry you. I just wanted to be beside him.

The pressure from my family.

My father's anger.

The fear of breaking everything.

But somehow, deep inside, I knew. If I didn't say it now if I didn't let him know how I felt I might lose him forever. So.....

"On the Train – Just Before Reaching Anna Nagar."

The train slowed as it approached the outskirts of the city. The landscape outside had changed but so had the silence between me and Siddharth.

I sat facing him now, my eyes a little glossy, my voice soft but steady. "*Siddharth- I have to tell you something, I said,* fingers nervously tracing the seam of the seat. "These four days... They've been the most beautiful days of my life."

Siddharth smiled gently, sensing something deeper behind my words.

I looked away for a moment, gathering strength. Then I met his eyes. *"I love you, Siddharth."* Truly. Completely. But... this isn't going to work. My Appa will never accept this. And I can't go against his word. He's already promised someone. I can't break him. I can't break myself either."

He stared at me in disbelief, pain flickering in his eyes. "What are you saying?"

I took a deep breath, fighting the tears. "You're such a good person. You deserve a life full of love, peace, and someone who can walk beside you freely. I want that for you, even if it's not with me."

His voice was barely a whisper. "Don't do this."

I placed my hand on his. I'll always be your best friend. And I'll always remember that someone loved me this deeply. I'm happy that Vijaya made this trip happen. Because in this life... I got to spend four days with you. And that means everything to me."

The train horn blew sharply as it approached Anna Nagar. I turned my face to the window, hiding the tears, knowing I had just broken my own heart for the sake of appa's promise.

I watched Siddharth step back.

I had heard the distance in his voice, I was sad.

"Moments Before the Train Stops."

The train began to slow, the screech of the brakes mirroring the ache tightening in my chest.

I had just told Siddharth goodbye not because I didn't love him, but because I loved my father more. I expected him to argue, maybe even walk away in pain. But Siddharth sat there for a long moment, eyes on me, steady.

He finally spoke, voice low but firm, "*I love you, Vellankanni.*" Nothing will ever change that. But I love *you* enough to respect what you believe in even if it tears me apart."

I blinked fast, my throat tightened.

He gently reached out and touched my hand, not to hold it forever but just to say one last thing. "I won't force you to fight with your family because even I don't want that. But know this: I'm not leaving because I've stopped loving you. I'm leaving *because you asked me to.* And even in that... I'll honor you."

The train came to a halt. The doors slid open. The noise of the station flooded in people, voices, announcements but in that moment, there was only silence between the two of us.

He helped me with my bags, walked beside me to the exit.

And when it was time to part, he didn't say goodbye.

He just said, "If not in this life… maybe the next."

And then he smiled. A broken smile. But a real one.

But in the little corner of that train, all was still.

"Vellankanni…"

Back in Anna Nagar , Finally, Siddharth managed to get a taxi. He made sure I was seated comfortably, and then he left. Meanwhile, I noticed that my phone suddenly had full network coverage. I thought of calling Amma, but within seconds, messages and calls started pouring in. Phones were lighting up like wildfire. On my screen, more than 35 missed calls and over 40 messages lit up at once. Social media was flooded with notifications popping up from every direction. My phone buzzed non-stop, as if the whole world had been trying to reach me all at once. Within seconds, I received a call from my college. The voice on the other end was firm: *"You have been rusticated from college."*

I was completely clueless. My mind went blank. What was happening? Why me? I couldn't make sense of any of it. Just then, Appa called. His voice was heavy stern, but with a hint of worry.

"Come home immediately," he said.

That was it. No explanation.

I was scared. My hands trembled slightly as I held the phone. I was still completely unaware of what had happened… and why everything was suddenly falling apart. Desperate for answers, I tried calling Vijaya but her number was unavailable. My heart sank. I dialed Arun next. His phone, too, was out of reach.

Panic slowly crept in. The silence from the people I trusted most was louder than anything else. Something was seriously wrong… and I was all alone in it. On the way home, I kept trying to call Siddharth. He was my last hope for some clarity. But no luck, his phone was switched off. Probably ran out of battery back on the train.

With each passing minute, the silence grew heavier. My mind raced with questions, fear, and worst-case scenarios. I had no idea what I was walking into. ChatApp groups, family chats, and Social stories were all buzzing with one name: *Vellankanni.*

Screenshots from the fake account were now circulating widely. Cousins were calling. Relatives were messaging. My Appa's phone hadn't stopped ringing.

Finally, Siddharth called. His voice was tense but steady.

"I just saw everything you're going viral on social media," he said. *"What's going on?"*

He was clearly upset with the situation, frustrated at how things had spiraled out of control. But one thing was certain, he never doubted me. *"I know you,"* he said firmly. *"You're a pure soul. Don't let this break you. I'm with you and so is my family."*

In that moment, his words felt like a lifeline in the middle of a storm. Someone still believed in me. That meant everything.

I finally reached home. The tension in the air was unbearable. Appa was on a call the man who was supposed to marry me had just called off the engagement.

"We're breaking this marriage," he had said bluntly, without even asking for the truth.

My parents were shattered. More than anger, I saw fear in their eyes, fear for my future, for my reputation, for what society would say.

And just then, Siddharth arrived with his mother. Appa was shocked but he stayed calm, and tears rolled out in Siddharth's arms.

Siddharth stood tall, calm but determined.

"Uncle, Aunty," he said, addressing my parents gently, *"please don't worry. Vellankanni is innocent. Whatever has happened, we are with her.*

I know who she is. And I will marry her, no matter what."

His mother nodded in agreement, her presence a quiet but strong reassurance.

For the first time that day, my parents' faces softened just a little. In the middle of everything crumbling, Siddharth stood like a pillar that refused to shake. Around 12:30 PM,

He turned to my parents and said firmly, *"Mom, Uncle, Aunty, Kalyani, Vellankanni please get ready. We're going to the police station. It's time to file a complaint."*

My father, usually so composed, looked shattered. His shoulders slumped, his eyes vacant. He didn't say much, just nodded slowly and got up.

He was heartbroken. This wasn't how he imagined his daughter's life unfolding. And now, instead of preparing for my wedding, he was heading to a police station tired, humiliated, and unsure of what lay ahead.

But Siddharth's presence gave us strength. In that moment, he wasn't just a friend or a fiancé he was the only one holding us together.

At the police station, we filed the complaint, hoping for some justice. But instead of sympathy or support, the officers laughed it off.

"What kind of upbringing is this? A girl like her, involved in such things?" one of them scoffed.

My father's face turned red with humiliation, and I could see the hurt in his eyes. They barely entertained us, dismissing our concerns as if they were nothing more than a nuisance.

"We can't help you. Leave," one of the officers said coldly.

As we walked back home, the silence between us was suffocating. My father's disappointment weighed heavily on my heart, and Siddharth, despite his strong exterior, seemed deeply troubled by the injustice. It felt like the world was crumbling around us, and no one cared to listen or understand.

As we started to leave, Siddharth stepped forward, his voice calm but insistent.

"Please, just listen to us. We need to file a proper complaint."

The officers sneered, but Siddharth didn't back down. He turned to one of the senior officers, who had been quietly observing the whole situation.

"Sir, I know this isn't easy, but we need your help. We're being wronged here."

For a moment, the officer hesitated, looking at the scene unfolding before him, my family, defeated and weary, and Siddharth, standing firm for what was right.

Finally, the senior officer nodded.

"Alright, I'll help you. Let's file the complaint properly."

A small sigh of relief escaped my lips. It wasn't much, but it was something. Maybe, just maybe, we weren't completely alone in this fight.

We left the police station, the weight of everything still heavy on our shoulders. I sat in the car with my parents, my younger sister, and Siddharth's mother. Appa was in the front seat, his eyes distant, while Siddharth sat beside him, keeping his focus on the road. Silence filled the car as we all sat there, lost in our thoughts, unsure of what would come next. Siddharth, trying to lighten the mood even a little, parked the car and got out to buy some food for everyone.

As the car came to a halt, I barely had a moment to relax when three men approached the vehicle. Without warning, they started pointing at me, their voices loud and mocking.

"She's the same girl from that viral video!" one of them laughed. Before I could react, they started teasing me and my family, hurling insults that stung more than I could explain. They had no idea what we were going through, no idea of the pain and humiliation we'd already faced.

To my shock, one of them pulled out their phone, started recording, and began making a reel intending to post it all over social media. They laughed as if it were all some sick joke, unaware that they were tearing my family apart even more.

As the men continued their cruel teasing, something shifted. Siddharth's mother and Amma, both shocked and angry, got out of the car. They approached the men, trying to defend us, to stop them from filming and mocking us further. But the situation was escalating quickly.

Just then, Siddharth arrived. Without a word, he stormed toward the men. In one swift motion, he shoved one of them to the ground, his fist connecting with his face with a force that silenced everything. The man stumbled back, clutching his nose, stunned and disoriented.

"Enough!" Siddharth barked. His voice was full of rage, the protective instinct in him roaring to life.

Without another second of hesitation, he turned to us, his eyes burning with anger but also with a resolve to protect.

"Let's go," he said, his voice steady now. We got in the car, and he drove off, leaving the stunned men behind.

The tension in the car was palpable. Siddharth had just stood up for us in a way no one else had, and for a brief moment, I felt safe again.

I switched off my phone, the constant buzzing and notifications too much to bear. My mind was racing, but I closed my eyes and leaned my head on Amma's shoulder, seeking some comfort, some escape from the chaos. The gentle motion of the car and the warmth of Amma's presence were the only things that kept me grounded.

Siddharth, on the other hand, was silent, his expressions were serious, helpless as he spoke with Appa. He tried reaching out to Arun and Vijaya, knowing they were still unaware of the storm that had hit us.

Vijaya woke up to an avalanche of notifications flooding her phone. Her screen was filled with messages, missed calls most of them from Siddharth. Confused, she rubbed her eyes, her heart racing as she scrolled through the endless updates.

The moment she clicked on one of the videos, her stomach dropped. There it was the viral video of *"Machi"*. She stared in disbelief, her hands trembling as she watched the footage of me being ridiculed, her heart sinking as she realized just how badly things had gone.

She immediately called Siddharth back, but his phone went straight to voicemail. Panic set in. What had she done? How had this spiral gone so far without her even knowing?

Her mind raced as the weight of her mistake hit her full force. She knew she couldn't stay where she was, not with this guilt hanging over her. Without thinking twice, she grabbed her things and ran out of her guesthouse, determined to fix the mess she had unwittingly contributed to.

While travelling back to Anna nagar she saw the video on social media, she was stunned and shocked beyond belief. She hadn't known how far the situation would escalate, how it would spiral out of control. The realization hit her like a wave, and she knew then just how much damage had been done.

Feeling a rush of guilt and regret, she couldn't stay still. Without a second thought, she ran from her house, desperate to find me, to apologize, to explain. She had to make things right. Her phone buzzed again. This time, it was a message from the hospital where she was admitted. She glanced at it absentmindedly, thinking it was just another update. But when she read it, her heart nearly stopped.

"Thank you, "Vellankanni, for donating O- blood. Our organization is deeply grateful to you for your generous contribution. - The Blood Donation Center."

{because I mentioned her number and details for donation}

The words seemed to echo in her mind. She hadn't known. She hadn't realized that while everything was unraveling for me, I had been quietly doing good, trying to help others in the midst of all the chaos. The guilt hit her like a punch to the gut.

"How could I have been so blind?" she thought, feeling worse with every passing second. She hadn't just misunderstood the situation; she had judged us without knowing the full truth, She was only jealous, without considering who I really was.

With the weight of that realization settling on her, Vijaya's steps quickened. She had to see me, had to apologize, and explain. She needed to make things right, even if she wasn't sure how.

As she walked, Vijaya's mind was racing, her guilt growing heavier with each step. The message from the hospital weighed on her more than anything else. She realized, in that moment, that I had saved her life donating blood during a time when she needed it most. She had no idea, that I had been the one behind that selfless act, all while she and others were so quick to judge me.

She couldn't carry this guilt anymore. She quickly dialed Siddharth's number, her hands shaking as she waited for him to pick up.

When he answered, his voice was filled with frustration. *Where are you? Vijaya's voice trembled as she spoke to Siddharth over the phone, the weight of her words pressing down on her.*

"Siddharth, I need to tell you something. It's… it's about Vellankanni,… I'm the one who created her social media account…I didn't know what I was doing at the time, but I did it. I pushed her into that world, Last night, In the overconsumption of alcohol…I don't know what happened, I wasn't thinking clearly."

Her words seemed to hang in the air for a long moment before she continued, her guilt consuming her with every syllable.

"Bro, I am wrong. Vellankanni is innocent in all this. I…I failed her. I'm so sorry."

Siddharth, who had been listening quietly, felt a rush of anger and frustration flood through him. He couldn't understand how things had spiraled so far out of control. But at the same time, he could hear the genuine remorse in Vijaya's voice, the recognition of her mistake.

Without a word, Siddharth's resolve grew stronger. He wasn't going to let this slide. "Vijaya," he said firmly, his voice cold, "You need to come over, Right now! Right now! You have to face her and apologize. This is bigger than just a conversation. We need to fix this mess." "Do you even realize what you've done? Her career and her entire life is in ruins because of you!" "Come home. Right now."

With tears in her eyes, she confessed her mistake again and again. *"Siddharth, I created her Social media ID, I am wrong. I misunderstood everything. I never knew what you were going through, what she was going through. I feel terrible… I should have been there for her, for you both."*

Her confession, "Vellankanni is the perfect child. She is beautiful, adored by her parents, and loved deeply by you. The brightest student in college, admired by everyone, Vellankanni seemed to have it all. *"I was jealous of everything she had. Her beauty, her family, you. Especially you. My life has never been like hers, and I just… I wanted to feel what it was like, even if it was all a lie."*

long silence,

"I didn't mean for things to go so far. I never meant to ruin her. I just wanted to feel seen, to matter for once. But I've hurt her, and I've hurt you too."

Siddharth (voice tight with anger)

"Vijaya, stop. Just stop talking."

(pause, a sharp breath)

"I can't believe this… You have to fix this."

(angrily, but measured)

"Come to Vellankanni's house. Right now. We're going to the police station. I need to see you face to face."

(final, firm)

"No more hiding. If you have any shred of decency left, you'll come. Now."

Siddharth's anger was palpable, but underneath it was a deep sadness. *"You need to come to her house right now. Apologize to her, and to her family. They've been through enough."*

Vijaya nodded, tears streaming down her face, and without wasting another moment, she rushed toward my house.

{Vijaya, on the other hand, was unraveling. Her life had never been perfect, not in love, not with her parents. The stark contrast between us consumed her with jealousy. She didn't just envy my life, she wanted it. So, in a desperate act, she created a fake account}.

When she arrived, the air was thick with tension. My parents, still processing everything that had happened, sat quietly. Siddharth stood beside me, his expression hard. He didn't speak, but his presence was a silent force of protection.

Vijaya, feeling the weight of her actions, stepped forward. Her voice was shaky as she looked at my parents first. *"I'm *so sorry. I can't even begin to imagine the pain I've caused. I am wrong about everything. I misunderstood her, I misunderstood all of you. And I'm deeply sorry for that."*

Vijaya (voice trembling, breaking down)

"I didn't even realize how deep it had gotten… the jealousy. It started after our birthday. That day, when I came to pick her up from her house… I saw everything."

(quiet pause, tears in her voice)

"Her amma was loving her so gently applying vibhuti on her forehead, kissing her like she was made of gold. Kalyani, gifting her something with so much pride. You… you loved her like she was the center of your world. And her appa, always making sure she was okay, like she was a queen in her own home."

(voice cracks)

"She had everything. And I, (long pause) I had nothing like that. Not love, not care, no siblings love, no father, not even a moment like that in my whole life." **"I'm a rebellious child… not because I wanted to be, but because no one ever taught me how to belong."**

(sobbing)

"So I did something unforgivable. I let the jealousy rot me from the inside, and I created that fake account. I wanted to make her feel what hate is all about. But what I did… it's not just wrong, it's a crime, it's sick. It hurt her. It hurt you."

(choking back guilt) "Punish me, Siddharth.

Punish me, Uncle, Aunty, Kalyani, I deserve it. Just don't think for a second that I don't know what I've done."

Then, she turned to me. Her eyes were filled with regret. *"Vellankanni, I… I failed you as a friend. "I failed Machi". I should have been there for you, and I wasn't. Please, forgive me."*

The room was silent for a long moment. It wasn't an easy forgiveness to grant, but her heartfelt apology hung in the air. The weight of everything was still there, but there was a flicker of hope that maybe, just maybe, things could begin to heal.

Vijaya knew that words alone wouldn't be enough to make things right. The damage had already been done, and she had to face the consequences of her actions. After deleting the fake social media account she had created, she took a deep breath, steeling herself for what was next.

She recorded a heartfelt video and posted it on her own social media. Her voice was shaky, but clear as she began to speak:

"I want to address the situation that has been affecting my dear friend, Vellankanni. I'm here to admit that everything that has happened, everything you've seen, is a result of my own jealousy, possessiveness, and… my own mistakes. In a moment of anger and overconsumption of alcohol, I misused social media and

caused irreparable damage to my friend's reputation and her family's peace."

Her eyes were filled with regret as she continued, speaking directly into the camera.

"I didn't realize the mess I was creating, the pain I was causing, until I saw the viral video. I let my emotions cloud my judgment, and I used a platform that shouldn't bring people together to tear someone down. I made a huge mistake, and for that, I am truly sorry."

She paused, her voice trembling as she said the words that weighed heavily on her heart:

"I accept full responsibility for what I did. I am handing myself over to the police, as I know that I have to face the consequences of my actions. I hurt my "Machi", and for that, I will forever regret what I've done."

With that, she posted the reel, "STOP-MACHI GOES VIRAL

#STOPMACHIGOESVIRA

#VELLANKANNI #JUSTICEFORVELANKANNI

her confession now out in the open for the world to see. As soon as it went live, messages poured in some supporting her, some angry, but the most important part was that she had owned up to her mistake.

Soon after Vijaya posted her heartfelt confession, the internet exploded again but this time, in a different way. The same phrase that once mocked me was now being shared with a new meaning.

"Later, the college also accepted me with great respect and expressed their apologies to my parents."

"AGAIN STOP, MACHI GOES VIRAL!"

This time, it trended with support.

Only now, it was followed by:

"Finally, Vellankanni got justice."
#finallyvellankannigotjusitice #machigoesviral

The tide had turned. People began to understand the truth. My name was no longer being dragged through the mud; it was being lifted, defended, respected. The pain we had endured was finally seen, and more importantly, acknowledged.

A few days later, I went to the police station with my parents, Siddharth, and his family. We had all been through enough. We requested the police to formally close the case. The senior officer, the one who had helped us when no one else would, respected our decision.

My parents, after much thought and silent conversations behind closed doors, decided to forgive Vijaya. They understood that children, especially friends make mistakes, and sometimes, those mistakes are heavier than they realize. As we stepped out of the police station, the sunlight felt warmer, softer like a quiet reassurance that the worst had passed.

I turned to look at Appa and Amma. For the first time in days, I saw something I had longed for peace on their faces. Appa's shoulders, once heavy with shame and worry, were finally relaxed. Amma held my hand tightly, her smile trembling with emotion. Their eyes met mine with pride not because everything had gone perfectly, but because we had endured together. And deep down, we all knew this healing, this strength it was all possible because of one person.

"Siddharth."

He stood beside me, not saying much, but his presence said everything. He had fought when I couldn't. He stood tall when everything around us collapsed. He gave my family the courage to breathe again. I looked at him, my eyes full of gratitude. Without him, none of this would have been possible.

And in that moment, surrounded by forgiveness, acceptance, and love, I realized that even in the middle of the deepest chaos, goodness can rise quietly, powerfully, and sometimes, in the form of someone who refuses to let go of your hand.

Vijaya stood, eyes full of remorse, her hands trembling slightly. She touched Amma's and Appa's feet, tears streaming down her cheeks. *"I'm sorry,"* she said quietly, *"for everything."*

Siddharth's mother placed a hand on her shoulder.

"It takes courage to accept your mistake like this, kutti. That's not easy. We forgive you."

I looked at her,

Vijaya my "MACHI", the girl who had hurt me the most, but who had also owned her mistake completely.

A part of me still ached, but I saw in her eyes the girl I used to know, the one who would have never intended to cause harm if she'd truly understood the weight of her actions.

I walked over, and in that quiet room, with everyone watching, I gave her a gentle nod.

"It hurt, Vijaya Machi. Deeply. But I see you now. And I forgive you."

She broke down in my arms, and for the first time in days, we all felt a quiet sense of closure settle in.

"To New Beginnings, and to Family."

A few days later, After Appa's announcement, the atmosphere at home was filled with a sense of anticipation. Appa, who had always been a man of few words, surprised me when he spoke up one evening.

"I want Siddharth and his mother to come over for dinner," Appa said with a smile, looking at Amma and me.

Amma's eyes lit up with happiness, and she quickly began making plans for the evening. We hadn't had a formal gathering in a while, and this dinner felt like a symbol of everything we had overcome. It was a way to seal the promise of new beginnings, to bridge the gap that had once existed between our families.

Later that evening, the doorbell rang, and there they were, Siddharth and his mother. Amma opened the door with a warm smile, welcoming them into our home. There was a slight tension in the air, but it wasn't uncomfortable. It was more of an unspoken acknowledgment that we were all part of something bigger now, a bond being formed between two families.

Dinner was set, and the house was filled with the delicious aroma of Amma's cooking. As we sat down to eat, the conversation flowed easily, breaking the initial ice. Appa, in his quiet but strong way, asked Siddharth's mother about her life, her work, and how she had raised such a remarkable son after his appa's death. His questions were thoughtful, respectful, and genuine, and I could see the warmth growing between them.

Siddharth's mother, who had always been supportive of him, spoke fondly of their close-knit family and how proud she was of him for standing by me through everything. He, who had always been the strong, silent type, found himself laughing along with us, his voice filled with genuine ease. He looked over at me occasionally, his eyes soft with affection.

As the evening wore on, I caught Appa looking at me and Siddharth with a knowing smile. It was a quiet moment of acceptance and understanding that, despite everything, love and respect had triumphed.

Amma, who was always the emotional heart of the house, raised her coffee glass toward Siddharth and his mother, saying with a smile, *"To new beginnings, and to family."*

And in that moment, I realized how far we had come. This dinner wasn't just about a meal. It was about healing, forgiveness, and the future we were building together. It was the beginning of a new chapter for all of us.

The air at home felt lighter, filled with a sense of calm that had been missing for far too long. Appa, who had remained silent for most of the week, finally gathered us all together in the living room. His eyes shone with a mix of pride and relief. He looked at Amma, then at me, and finally turned to Siddharth, who had stood by us every step of the way.

Appa cleared his throat, his voice steady but filled with emotion as he spoke, *"I've seen a lot these past few days. I've seen the strength in my daughter, and I've seen the loyalty and integrity in Siddharth."* He paused, as if carefully choosing his words. *"After their boards, and once they've chosen their careers, I will make sure that Siddharth becomes my son-in-law."*

The words felt like a dream come true. I looked at Siddharth, who seemed as surprised as I was, though I could see a quiet happiness in his eyes. He had never asked for approval, never needed it, but hearing those words from Appa meant everything.

"Siddharth, you have proven yourself to be someone worthy of our family," Appa continued, his voice filled with pride. *"I'm happy to welcome you as my son-in-law. "And I'm sorry, Siddharth, for the way I behaved. I know I may have crossed a line, but I was only trying to protect my daughter. One day, when you become the father of a daughter, you'll understand why and what I did. "I trust you to protect and support my daughter, and I know she will find happiness with you."* Tears welled up in my eyes as I looked at Siddharth. It wasn't just about marriage it was about the bond, the respect, and the love that had formed between us and our families through all of this.

Siddharth smiled warmly at my parents, his respect for them evident.

"Thank you, Uncle. Thank you, Aunty. I promise to always care for Vellankanni and support her dreams."

And with that, the chapter closed on a storm of pain, and a new chapter opened one of healing, hope, and love.

MORAL OF THE STORY

"Use social media wisely."

This is a reminder to today's youth about the immense power and responsibility that comes with using social media. What begins as a moment of fun, jealousy, or carelessness can quickly spiral into irreversible consequences that hurt lives, families, and reputations.

Social media can be a tool for connection, awareness, and positivity but in the wrong hands, or used without thought, it can become a weapon. Misusing it, spreading false information, or violating someone's dignity is not just wrong, it can be a serious *crime.*

So, to every young heart reading this: **"Use social media wisely."** Think before you post, before you share, before you judge. Protect your integrity and respect others'. A single action online can have a lasting impact offline.

Let's build a world where technology uplifts—not destroys.

– Shveta Iyer

A Message to the Youth

In today's fast-paced world, social media has become more than just a platform. It's our voice, our identity, and sometimes, our mirror. But with great power comes great responsibility.

Machi Goes Viral is not just a story. It's a reminder to the youth.

A reminder that while social media can connect, empower, and inspire, it can also mislead, hurt, and even destroy if used carelessly.

- What you post today can impact your future.
- What goes viral may not always be your truth.
- And sometimes, what seems like fun can actually be a digital crime.

This book aims to gently, yet firmly, raise awareness among young readers about the advantages and disadvantages of social media. It encourages you to ask,

- Are you protecting your privacy?
- Are you lifting others up or tearing them down?
- Are you using your platform to build, not break?

Use social media wisely.

In a world that's watching, choose to be kind.

Choose to be thoughtful.

Choose to be responsible.

Create better!

Because your story matters. And how you share it matters even more.

#machigoesviral

#shvetaiyer

"I extend my sincere gratitude to my college friends for being an integral part of my journey."

- Manish
- Nandkishore
- Bhasker
- Abhijeet
- Dnyanesh
- Neelam
- Vidula
- Madhuri
- Kavita
- Rajul K

#machigoesviral

#shvetaiyer